삼포 가는 길

아시아에서는 《바이링궐 에디션 한국 대표 소설》을 기획하여 한국의 우수한 문학을 주제별로 엄선해 국내외 독자들에게 소개합니다. 이 기획은 국내외 우수한 번역가들이 참여하여 원작의 품격을 최대한 살렸습니다. 문학을 통해 아시아의 정체성과 가치를 살피는 데 주력해 온 아시아는 한국인의 삶을 넓고 깊게 이해하는 데 이 기획이 기여하기를 기대합니다.

Asia Publishers presents some of the very best modern Korean literature to readers worldwide through its new Korean literature series 〈Bilingual Edition Modern Korean Literature〉. We are proud and happy to offer it in the most authoritative translation by renowned translators of Korean literature. We hope that this series helps to build solid bridges between citizens of the world and Koreans through a rich in-depth understanding of Korea.

바이링궐 에디션 한국 대표 소설 007
Bi-lingual Edition Modern Korean Literature 007

The Road to Sampo

황석영
삼포 가는 길

Hwang Sok-yong

ASIA
PUBLISHERS

Contents

삼포 가는 길
The Road to Sampo

영달은 어디로 갈 것인가 궁리해 보면서 잠깐 서 있었다. 새벽의 겨울바람이 매섭게 불어왔다. 밝아 오는 아침 햇빛 아래 헐벗은 들판이 드러났고, 곳곳에 얼어붙은 시냇물이나 웅덩이가 반사되어 빛을 냈다. 바람 소리가 먼 데서부터 몰아쳐서 그가 섰는 창공을 베면서 지나갔다. 가지만 남은 나무들이 수십여 그루씩 들판가에서 바람에 흔들렸다.

그가 넉 달 전에 이곳을 찾았을 때에는 한참 추수기에 이르러 있었고 이미 공사는 막판이었다. 곧 겨울이 오게 되면 공사가 새봄으로 연기될 테고 오래 머물 수 없으리라는 것을 그는 진작부터 예상했던 터였다. 아니나 다를

Yŏng-dal stopped in order to try to decide which road to take. The cold winter wind was especially sharp at the break of day. As the sun rose across the scraggy fields, the frozen streams and puddles, lying about here and there, threw back glints of sunlight. The wind blowing from afar passed overhead, cutting through the air above him. The bare trees standing in clumps at the edge of the plotted fields shook in the wind.

He came here four months ago during the harvest time. The construction season was drawing near to an end. Winter was not for off. The construction would come to a stop only to resume in the spring. He

까, 현장 사무소가 사흘 전에 문을 닫았고, 영달이는 밥집에서 달아날 기회만 노리고 있었던 것이다.

누군가 밭고랑을 지나 걸어오고 있었다. 해가 떠서 음지와 양지의 구분이 생기자 언덕의 그림자나 숲의 그늘로 가려진 곳에서는 언 흙이 부서지는 버석이는 소리가 들렸으나 해가 내리쪼인 곳은 녹기 시작하여 붉은 흙이 질척해 보였다. 다가오는 사람이 숲 그늘을 벗어났는데 신발 끝에 벌겋게 붙어 올라온 진흙 뭉치가 걸을 때마다 뒤로 몇 점씩 흩어지고 있었다. 그는 길가에 우두커니 서서 담배를 태우고 있는 영달이 쪽을 보면서 왔다. 그는 키가 훌쩍 크고 영달이는 작달막했다. 그는 팽팽하게 불러 오른 맹꽁이 배낭을 한쪽 어깨에 느슨히 걸쳐 메고 머리에는 개털 모자를 귀까지 가려 쓰고 있었다. 검게 물들인 야전 잠바의 깃 속에 턱이 반나마 파묻혀서 누군지 쌍통을 알아볼 도리가 없었다. 그는 몇 걸음 남겨 놓고 서더니 털모자의 챙을 이마빡에 붙도록 척 올리면서 말했다.

“천 씨네 집에 기시던 양반이군.”

영달이도 낯이 익은 서른댓 되어 보이는 사내였다. 공사장이나 마을 어귀의 주막에서 가끔 지나친 적이 있는 얼굴이었다.

would have to leave. Three days ago they closed the construction office as he had expected. Now he was looking for an opportunity to sneak out the canteen where he'd been staying and eating.

He saw a person coming in his direction across the fields on which the sun made a checkered pattern of light and shade. One could hear the frozen earth breaking in the shade, while the red earth melted in the sun. The approaching figure came out from behind the shaded darkness of the trees. The dough of red clay came off his footgear, as he walked towards Yŏng-dal who stood vacantly by the wayside, smoking a cigarette. He was a tall man in sharp contrast to Yŏng-dal's short figure. The canvas sack that looked like a frog's belly, as it was filled to the brim, was hanging loosely from his shoulder, and there was a dog-fur hat on his head with the earflaps pulled down over his ears. It was hard to tell who he was, as the turned-up collar of his army field jacket came up to his cheeks. He walked up to Yŏng-dal, until he was only a few paces away from Yŏng-dal, and said, pushing the brim of his hat upright:

"So you are the one who used to stay at Ch'ŏn's place, aren't you?"

"아까 존 구경 했시다."

그는 털모자를 잠근 단추를 여느라고 턱을 치켜들었다. 그러고 나서 비행사처럼 양쪽 빰으로 귀가리개를 늘어뜨리면서 빙긋 웃었다.

"천가란 사람, 거품을 물구 마누라를 개 패듯 때려잡던데."

영달이는 그를 쏘아보며 우물거렸다.

"내…… 그런 촌놈은 참."

"거 병신 안 됐는지 몰라. 머리채를 질질 끌구 마당에 나와선 차구 짓밟구…… 야, 그 사람 환장한 모양이더군."

이건 누굴 엿 먹이느라구 수작질인가, 하는 생각이 들어서 불끈했지만 영달이는 애써 참으며 담뱃불이 손가락 끝에 닿도록 쭈욱 빨아 넘겼다. 사내가 손을 내밀었다.

"불 좀 빌립시다."

"버리슈."

담배꽁초를 건네주며 영달이가 퉁명스럽게 말했다. 하긴 창피한 노릇이었다. 밥값을 떼고 달아나서가 아니라, 역에 나갔던 천가 놈이 예상 외로 이른 시각인 다섯 시쯤 돌아왔고 현장에서 덜미를 잡혔던 것이었다. 그는 옷만 간신히 추스르고 나와서 천가가 분풀이로 청주댁을 후려

Yŏng-dal recognized the face. He came across this man of about thirty years of age several times at the construction site, on the village roads, and in the taverns.

"I really enjoyed the scene, by the way," he continued. He thrust up his chin to unbutton the earflaps tied under it, and let the flaps hang loose like an airplane pilot.

Smiling, he said: "Ch'ŏn sure gave his wife a real beating—as if he was beating a dog."

Yŏng-dal looked straight at him and mumbled indistinctly: "That stupid bastard."

"He might have crippled her for life, I don't know—dragging her out by the hair to the backyard, kicking, and trampling like that," said the man. "Wow, he looked—crazy."

"What is he doing," Yŏng-dal thought, "trying to make a fool out of me?" Though he felt anger swelling up in his throat, he controlled himself and inhaled the smoke, puffing hard at the cigarette stump, until it burned down almost to his fingertips.

The man in the dog-fur hat put out his hand, asking, "May I?"

Handing him the butt of the cigarette, Yŏng-dal said gruffly, "You can throw it away." It was a

패는 동안 방아실에 숨어 있었다. 영달이는 변명 삼아 혼잣말 비슷이 중얼거렸다.

“계집 탓할 거 있수 사내 잘못이지.”

“시골 아낙네 치군 드물게 날씬합디다. 모두들 발랑 까졌다구 하지만서두.”

“여자야 그만이었죠. 처녀 적에 군용차두 탔답디다. 고생 많이 한 여자요.”

“바가지한테 세금두 내구, 거기두 줬겠구만.”

“뭐요? 아니 이 양반이…….”

사내가 입김을 길게 내뿜으며 껄껄 웃어젖혔다.

“거 왜 그러시나. 아, 재미 본 게 댁뿐인 줄 아쇼? 오다가다 만난 계집에 너무 일심 품지 마셔.”

녀석의 말버릇이 시종 그렇게 나오니 드러내 놓고 화를 내기도 뭣해서 영달이는 픽 웃고 말았다. 개피떡이나 인절미를 전방으로 호송되는 군인들께 팔았다는 것인데 딴은 열차를 타며 사내들 틈을 누비던 계집이 살림을 한답시고 들어앉아 절름발이 천가 여편네 노릇을 하려니 따분했을 것이었다. 공사장 인부들이나 떠돌이 장사치를 끌어들여 하숙도 치고 밥도 파는 사람인데, 사내 재미까지 보려는 눈치였다. 영달이 눈에 청주댁이 예사로 보였을 리

shameful business, he thought, as he looked back upon the incident. Not that he minded running away without paying off the debt he'd been drawing at Ch'ŏn's canteen for his meals. He didn't expect Ch'ŏn to be back so early from the railway station, at 5 A.M., to catch him in bed with his wife. He could scarcely collect his clothes and ran out the door, until he hid in the mill-room, where he listened to Ch'ŏn beating up his wife.

"It wasn't her fault, but his," Yŏng-dal muttered, as if he was excusing himself.

"The woman looked too good for an out-of-the-way place like that," said the other man, "although everybody said that she had too easy a manner."

"She was a good girl," Yŏng-dal said. "I heard she worked on the army trains as a young girl. She had a hard life."

"She must have paid her dues to the M.P.s," said the other men.

"What the hell do you mean by that?" As Yŏng-dal flared up, the man in the dog-fur hat burst out laughing. White mist came out of his mouth as he laughed. "Don't be foolish. You are not the only one who had a good time with her. You shouldn't get too serious about such a girl."

만무했다. 까무잡잡한 얼굴에 곱게 치떠서 흘기는 눈길하며, 밤이면 문밖에 나가 앉아 하염없이 불러대는 〈흑산도 아가씨〉라든가, 어쨌든 나중엔 거의 환장할 지경이었다.

"얼마나 있었소?"

사내가 물었다. 가까이 얼굴을 맞대고 보니 그리 흉악한 몰골도 아니었고, 우선 그 시원시원한 태도가 은근히 밉질 않다고 영달이는 생각했다. 그가 자기보다는 몇 살쯤 더 나이 들어 보였다. 그리고 이 바람 부는 겨울 들판에 척 걸터앉아서도 만사태평인 꼴이었다. 영달이는 처음보다는 경계하지 않고 대답했다.

"넉 달 있었소. 그런데 노형은 어디루 가쇼?"

"삼포에 갈까 하오."

사내는 눈을 가늘게 뜨고 조용히 말했다. 영달이가 고개를 흔들었다.

"방향 잘못 잡았수. 거긴 벽지나 다름없잖소. 이런 겨울철에."

"내 고향이오."

사내가 목장갑 낀 손으로 코밑을 쓱 훔쳐 냈다. 그는 벌써 들판 저 끝을 바라보고 있었다. 영달이와는 전혀 사정이 달라진 것이다. 그는 집으로 가는 중이었고, 영달이는

As the other man insisted on easy manners, Yŏng-dal couldn't stay angry. He smiled. The woman used to sell rice-cakes to the soldiers on the army trains, she once told him. It must have been difficult for a girl who led a life like that to settle down to the dull job of being the wife of a cripple like Ch'ŏn. She started taking in construction workers and peddlers as lodgers, who perhaps were also her lovers. Yŏng-dal couldn't help noticing her seductiveness. Her dark complexion, the way she looked at him from the corner of her eyes, "Girl from Huksando" that she would sing wistfully, sitting at the gate of her house—all these things worked an irresistible magic on him.

"How long did you live there?" asked the man in the dog-fur hat. At close range, he didn't look as rough as he did before. In fact, Yŏng-dal thought he liked his straightforward openness. More likely than not, the man was five years or so older than Yŏng-dal. Sitting on the ground by him, he was completely at ease in these bleak winter fields. Lowering his guard, Yŏng-dal said, "Four months. Where are you heading?"

"To Sampo—I think," said the other man calmly, looking at him through his half-closed eyes.

또 다른 곳으로 달아나는 길 위에 서 있었기 때문이었다.

"참…… 집에 가는군요."

사내가 일어나 맹꽁이 배낭을 한쪽 어깨에다 걸쳐 메면서 영달이에게 물었다.

"어디 무슨 일자리 찾아가쇼?"

"댁은 오라는 데가 있어서 여기 왔었소? 언제나 마찬가지죠."

"자, 난 이제 가 봐야겠는걸."

그는 뒤도 돌아보지 않고 질척이는 둑길을 향해 올라갔다. 그가 둑 위로 올라서더니 배낭을 다른 편 어깨 위로 바꾸어 메고는 다시 하반신부터 차례로 개털 모자 끝까지 둑 너머로 사라졌다. 영달이는 어디로 향하겠다는 별 뾰족한 생각도 나지 않았고, 동행도 없이 길을 갈 일이 아득했다. 가다가 도중에 헤어지게 되더라도 우선은 말동무라도 있었으면 싶었다. 그는 멍청히 섰다가 잰걸음으로 사내의 뒤를 따랐다. 영달이는 둑 위로 뛰어 올라갔다. 사내의 걸음이 무척 빨라서 벌써 차도로 나가는 샛길에 접어들어 있었다. 차도 양쪽에 대빗자루를 거꾸로 박아 놓은 듯한 앙상한 포플러들이 줄을 지어 섰는 게 보였다. 그는 둑 아래로 달려 내려가며 사내를 불렀다.

Yŏng-dal shook his head. "That's not a good place to go. Such an out-of-the-way place. Especially in winter like this."

"But that's my home town," said the man as he wiped his mouth with his gloved hand. He looked towards the far side of the fields. His situation was the complete opposite of Yŏng-dal's; he was going home and Yŏng-dal was on the run—to another strange place.

"So you are going home," said Yŏng-dal.

The man stood up and slung up the frog-belly canvas sack on his shoulder. He asked Yŏng-dal, "Any particular job you have in mind?"

"You didn't come here yourself, because a job was waiting for you, did you?" retorted Yŏng-dal. "Isn't it always the case?"

"Well, I must be on my way." The man didn't even look back as he walked away towards the bank of the stream. He climbed onto the bank, changed his sack to the other shoulder and started down the other side. He disappeared over the bank, first the lower part of his body and eventually the tip of his dog-fur hat. Yŏng-dal stood at a loss for a while, unable to decide upon a particular direction or road to take. What he needed was a fellow traveller. It

"여보쇼, 노형!"

그가 멈춰 서더니 뒤를 돌아보고 나서 다시 천천히 걸어갔다. 영달이는 달려가서 그 뒤편에 따라붙어 헐떡이면서,

"같이 갑시다. 나두 월출리까진 같은 방향인데……."

했는데도 그는 대답이 없었다. 영달이는 그의 뒤통수에다 대고 말했다.

"젠장, 이런 겨울은 처음이오. 작년 이맘때는 좋았지요. 월 삼천 원짜리 방에서 작부랑 살림을 했으니까. 엄동설한에 정말 갈 데 없이 빳빳하게 됐는데요."

"우린 습관이 되어 놔서."

사내가 말했다.

"삼포가 여기서 몇 린 줄 아쇼? 좌우간 바닷가까지만도 몇 백 리 길이오. 거기서 또 배를 타야 해요."

"몇 년 만입니까?"

"십 년이 넘었지. 가 봤자…… 아는 이두 없을 거요."

"그럼 뭣하러 가쇼?"

"그냥…… 나이 드니까, 가 보구 싶어서."

그들은 차도로 들어섰다. 자갈과 진흙으로 다져진 길이 그런대로 걷기에 편했다. 영달이는 시린 손을 잠바 호주머니에 처박고 연방 꼼지락거렸다.

would be better, even if the company lasted just for a little while—just somebody to talk to, while he was on the road. Coming out of his bemusement, Yŏng-dal hurriedly followed the man who had just disappeared beyond the river bank. As he reached the top of the bank, he could see the man in the dog-fur hat walking very fast in the distance. He was already entering the path leading to the roadway lined with two symmetrical columns of poplars, looking like bamboo brooms standing upside down. As he ran down the bank, Yŏng-dal called out, "Hey, you there!"

The man in the dog-fur hat paused a moment and turned around, but then kept on walking, Yŏng-dal ran after him. When he caught up with him, he said, gasping for breath, "Let's go together. I'm going in the same direction as you are, at least up to Wŏlchul."

The man did not answer.

"Damn it. I never saw a winter like this," Yŏng-dal spoke again to the back of the other man's head. "It was good last winter. We had a room, three thousand won a month, me and the barmaid with whom I lived. This winter is terrible. Frozen stiff, that's what I may become any moment now."

"어이, 육실허게는 춥네. 바람만 안 불면 좀 낫겠는데."

사내는 별로 추위를 타지 않았는데, 털모자와 야전잠바로 단단히 무장한 탓도 있겠지만 원체가 혈색이 건강해 보였다. 사내가 처음으로 다정하게 영달이에게 물었다.

"어떻게 아침은 자셨소?"

"웬걸요."

영달이가 열쩍게 웃었다.

"새벽에 몸만 간신히 빠져나온 셈인데……."

"나두 못 먹었소. 찬샘까진 가야 밥술이라두 먹게 될 거요. 진작에 떴을걸. 이젠 겨울에 움직일 생각이 안 납디다."

"인사 늦었네요. 나 노영달이라구 합니다."

"나는 정가요."

"우리두 기술이 좀 있어 놔서 일자리만 잡으면 별 걱정 없지요."

영달이가 정 씨에게 빌붙지 않을 뜻을 비쳤다.

"알고 있소. 착암기 잡지 않았소? 우리넨, 목공에 용접에 구두까지 수선할 줄 압니다."

"야 되게 많네. 정말 든든하시겠구만."

"십 년이 넘었다니까."

"Well, one gets used to that sort of thing," said the other man. "Do you have any idea how far Sampo is? At least several hundred li, that is, to the sea coast, and then we have to take a boat."

"How long has it been since you left Sampo?" asked Yŏng-dal.

"Over ten years," answered the other man, and he continued, "There won't be anybody who will recognize me there."

"Why do you want to go back then?" asked Yŏng-dal.

"For no particular reason," said the other man. "As I'm getting old, I just feel like visiting it."

The two men turned onto the roadway. It was easier to walk on the street, as the road was covered with gravel and clay. Yŏng-dal kept his hands in his pockets. He constantly worked them to keep them warm as best as he could. "So damned cold! If only there was no wind," he said.

The man in the dog-fur hat did not seem to feel as cold as Yŏng-dal did. It was true that he was heavily dressed with a fur hat and a field jacket, but he also looked unusually healthy and robust. He spoke to Yŏng-dal, showing some warmth for the first time: "Did you eat anything for breakfast?"

"그래도 어디서 그런 걸 배웁니까?"

"다 좋은 데서 가르치고 내보내는 집이 있지."

"나두 그런 데나 들어갔으면 좋겠네."

정 씨가 쓴웃음을 지으며 고개를 저었다.

"지금이라두 쉽지. 하지만 집이 워낙에 커서 말요."

"큰집……."

하다 말고 영달이는 정 씨의 얼굴을 쳐다봤다. 정 씨는 고개를 밑으로 숙인 채로 묵묵히 걷고 있었다. 언덕을 넘어섰다. 길이 내리막이 되면서 강변을 따라서 먼 산을 돌아 나간 모양이 아득하게 보였다. 인가가 좀처럼 보이지 않는 황량한 들판이었다. 마른 갈대밭이 헝클어진 채 휘청대고 있었고 강 건너 곳곳에 모래바람이 일어나는 게 보였다. 정 씨가 말했다.

"저 산을 넘어야 찬샘골인데. 강을 질러가는 게 빠르겠군."

"단단히 얼었을까."

강물은 꽁꽁 얼어붙어 있었다. 얼음이 녹았다가 다시 얼곤 해서 우툴두툴한 표면이 그리 미끄럽지는 않았다. 바람이 불어, 깨어진 살얼음 조각들을 날려 그들의 얼굴을 따갑게 때렸다.

"No," Yŏng-dal smiled shame-facedly. "I could barely make my escape in the dark."

"I haven't eaten yet myself," said the other man, but we'll have to wait at least until we get to Chansaem. I should have left earlier this morning. I'm now getting to the age when one doesn't like moving in winter."

"I didn't introduce myself. My name is No Yŏng-dal," said Yŏng-dal.

"I am Chŏng." The other man gave him his family name.

"I know how to work machinery. Once I get a job, I'll have nothing to worry about him," said Yŏng-dal to let Chŏng know that he had no intention of sucking around.

"I know," said Chŏng. "Didn't you work with the rock-drill? As for me, I can do carpentry, welding, and cobbling."

"Wow, having all those skills, you must feel very secure," Yŏng-dal said admiringly.

"I've been doing them for more than ten years," said Chŏng.

"Where did you learn them?" asked Yŏng-dal.

"There's a very nice place where they teach you all those skills," answered the other man.

"차라리, 저쪽 다릿목에서 버스나 기다릴 걸 잘못했나 봐요."

숨을 헉헉 들이켜던 영달이가 투덜대자 정 씨가 말했다.

"자주 끊겨서 언제 올지두 모르오. 그보다두 현금을 아껴야지. 굶어두 돈 있으면 든든하니까."

"하긴 그래요."

"월출 가면 남행열차를 탈 수는 있소. 거기서 기차 타려오?"

"뭐…… 돼 가는 대루. 그런데 삼포는 어느 쪽입니까?"

정 씨가 막연하게 남쪽 방향을 턱짓으로 가리켰다.

"남쪽 끝이오."

"사람이 많이 사나요, 삼포라는 데는?"

"한 열 집 살까? 정말 아름다운 섬이오. 비옥한 땅은 남아돌아가구, 고기두 얼마든지 잡을 수 있구 말이지."

영달이가 얼음 위로 미끄럼을 지치면서 말했다.

"야아 그럼, 거기 가서 아주 말뚝을 박구 살아 버렸으면 좋겠네."

"조오치. 하지만 댁은 안 될걸."

"어째서요."

"타관 사람이니까."

"I wish I could go there," said Yŏng-dal naively.

But Chŏng said with a bitter smile, shaking his head: "It's easy to go there, but I'm not sure you would really want to go. It is a very big place—only too big."

"Too big?" Yŏng-dal stopped in the middle of his sentence and looked at Chŏng's face. Chŏng was walking steadily in silence, with his face lowered a bit. The uphill road became a downhill road. Below them, they could see the road winding along a stream and distant fields. The winter fields lay bleak with hardly a farmer's hut as far as the eye could see. The dry rushes swayed in tangled confusion and the wind whirled up sands on the other side of the stream.

"The village of Chansaem lies over that mountain there," said Chŏng. "We had better cut across the stream if we want to make better time."

"Do you think it is frozen solid enough?" asked Yŏng-dal.

The stream was, in fact, frozen very solid. The ice was rough and not slippery, the water having frozen over several times after repeated freezing and melting. The wind picked up loose bits of ice and slapped the two men hard in the face.

그들은 얼어붙은 강을 건넜다. 구름이 몰려들고 있었다.

"눈이 올 거 같군. 길 가기 힘들어지겠소."

정 씨가 회색으로 흐려 가는 하늘을 걱정스럽게 올려다 보았다. 산등성이로 올라서자 아래쪽에 작은 마을의 집들이 점점이 흩어져 있는 게 한눈에 들어왔다. 가물거리는 지붕 위로 간신히 알아볼 만큼 가느다란 연기가 엷게 퍼져 흐르고 있었다. 교회의 종탑도 보였고 학교 운동장도 보였다. 기다란 철책과 철조망이 연이어져 마을 뒤의 온 들판을 둘러싸고 있는 것도 보였다. 군대의 주둔지인 듯했는데, 마을은 마치 그 철책의 끝에 간신히 매어 달려 있는 것 같았다.

그들은 읍내로 들어갔다. 다과점도 있었고, 극장, 다방, 당구장, 만물상점 그리고 주점이 장터 주변에 여러 채 붙어 있었다. 거리는 아침이라서 아직 조용했다. 그들은 어느 읍내에나 있는 서울식당이란 주점으로 들어갔다. 한 뚱뚱한 여자가 큰솥에다 우거짓국을 끓이고 있었고 주인인 듯한 사내와 동네 청년 둘이 떠들어대고 있었다.

"나는 전연 눈치를 못 챘다구. 옷을 한 가지씩 빼어다 따루 보따리를 싸 놨던 모양이라."

"새벽에 동네를 빠져나간 게 틀림없습니다."

"Perhaps we should have waited for the bus by the bridge," gasped Yŏng-dal, out of breath from walking too fast.

"The buses are never on time," said Chŏng. "Besides, we must watch where our money goes. Even when you haven't eaten, it feels good and secure to have money on you."

"You're right," agreed Yŏng-dal.

"At Wŏlchul we can take a southbound train," said Chŏng. "Are you going south or what?"

"I had better wait and see," Yŏng-dal hesitated. "Which way is Sampo?"

"South, that is, as far south as you can go," said Chŏng, vaguely pointing his chin to the south.

"How big a place is that? Are there many people living there?" asked Yŏng-dal.

"Ten houses or so," explained Chŏng. "It's a pretty island, Sampo is. The soil is good, lots of land. Fishing is good, too. You can catch as much fish as you want."

"If it's as good as you say, why not pitch our tents there and call it home?" said Yŏng-dal, skating over the ice on the road.

"Why not, indeed?" said Chŏng. "But not you."

"Why not?" Yŏng-dal looked up.

"어젯밤에 윤 하사하구 긴 밤을 잔다구 그래서, 뒷방에서 늦잠 자는 줄 알았지 뭔가."

"새벽에 윤 하사가 부대루 들어가자마자 튄 겁니다."

"옷값에 약값에 식비에…… 돈이 보통 들어간 줄 아나, 빚만 해두 자그마치 오만 원이거든."

영달이와 정 씨가 자리에 앉자 그들은 잠깐 얘기를 멈추고 두 낯선 사람들의 행색을 살펴보았다. 영달이는 연탄난로 위에 두 손을 내려뜨리고 비벼대면서 불을 쪼였다. 정 씨가 털모자를 벗으면서 말했다.

"국밥 둘만 말아 주쇼."

"네, 좀 늦어져두 별일 없겠죠?"

뚱뚱한 여자가 국솥에서 얼굴을 들고 미리 웃음으로 얼버무리며 양해를 구했다.

"좌우간 맛있게만 말아 주쇼."

여자가 국자를 요란하게 놓고는 한숨을 내리쉬었다.

"개쌍년 같으니!"

정 씨도 영달이처럼 난로를 통째로 껴안을 듯이 바싹 다가앉아서 여자를 물끄러미 올려다보았다.

"색시가 도망을 쳤지 뭐예요. 그래서 불도 꺼졌고, 국거리도 없어서 인제 막 시작을 했답니다."

"Because you're not a native."

The two men crossed the frozen stream. Clouds were gathering in the sky.

"It's going to snow," observed Chŏng. "The going will get tougher." He looked up at the sky, turning grey, with misgivings. Standing on the mountain ridge, they could see the houses in the village below. Above the houses the smoke was rising, barely visible, and spreading sideways. There were a church steeple and the open space of a school playground. On the farther side of the village ran an iron fence and barbed wire enclosing a tract of land. It appeared to be a military base to which the village was attached like an insignificant appendage.

They walked into the village. It had just about everything—a pastry shop, a theatre, a coffee house, a pool room, a general store, a saloon and a marketplace. But it was still too early in the morning and the streets were deserted. They entered a drinking house with the sign, "Seoul Restaurant," which one could find any small town around these days. A fat woman was stirring cabbage soup in the iron pot. A man who looked like the owner and two local young men were talking excitedly. "I hadn't suspected anything," said

하고 나서 여자가 남자들에게 외쳤다.

"아니 근데 당신들은 뭘 앉아서 콩이네 팥이네 하구 있는 거예요? 냉큼 가서 잡아오지 못하구선. 얼마 달아나지 못했을 테니 따라가서 머리채를 끌구 와요."

주인 남자가 주눅이 든 목소리로 대답했다.

"필요 없네. 아무래도 월출서 기차를 탈 테니까 정거장 목만 지키면 된다구."

"그럼 자전거 타구 빨리 가서 기다려요."

"이거 원 날씨가 이렇게 추워서야."

"무슨 얘기예요. 그 백화라는 년이 돈 오만 원이란 말요."

마을 청년이 끼어들었다.

"서울식당이 원래 백화 땜에 호가 났던 거 아닙니까. 그 애가 장사는 그만이었죠."

"군인들이 백화라면, 군화까지 팔아서라두 술을 마실 정도였으니까."

뚱뚱이 여자가 빈정거렸다.

"웃기네, 그래 봤자 지가 똥갈보라. 내 장사 수완 덕이지 뭐. 그년 요새 좀 아프다는 핑계루…… 이건 물을 긷나, 밥을 제대루 하나, 손님을 받나, 소용없어. 그년두 육

one of them. "She must have taken her clothes, piece by piece, and had stashed them in some secret place."

"She must have sneaked away early in the morning."

"She said that she was having an 'all-nighter' with Sergeant Yun," another said. "I thought she was sleeping late in the backroom because of that."

"She must have sneaked away right after Sergeant Yun went back to the base early in the morning."

"The money she owed me for her clothes, her medicine, her meals..." said the owner, "it's not just a small sum that she owes me. It's no less than fifty thousand won."

When Yŏng-dal and Chŏng took seats at a table, they stopped talking and tried to size them up. Yŏng-dal spread out his hands towards the coal stove to warm them, rubbing them together.

"Two boiled rice in soup, please," called out Chŏng, taking off his hat.

"Do you mind waiting a bit?" asked the fat woman who was stirring the soup, looking up and a smiling apologetically.

"That's all right as long as you make it good and tasty," answered Chŏng.

개월이면 찬샘 바닥서 진이 모조리 빠진 거예요. 빚이나 뽑아내면 참한 신마이루 기리까이 할려던 참이었어. 아, 뭘 해요? 빨리 가서 역을 지키라니까."

마누라의 호통에 주인 사내가 깜짝 놀란 듯이 어깨를 움츠렸다.

"알았대니까……."

"얼른 갔다 와요. 내 대포 한턱 쓸게."

남자들 셋이 우르르 밀려 나갔다. 정 씨가 중얼거렸다.

"젠장, 그 백화 아가씨라두 있었으면 술이나 옆에서 쳐 달랠걸."

"큰일예요, 글쎄. 저녁마다 장정들이 몰려오는데……."

"아가씨 서넛은 있어야지."

"색시 많이 두면 공연히 번거러워요. 이런 데서야 반반한 애 하나면 실속이 있죠, 모자라면 꿔다 앉히구…… 왜 좀 놀다 갈려우? 내 불러다 주께."

"왜 이러슈, 먼 길 가는 사람이 아침부터 주색 잡다간 저녁에 이 마을서 장사 지내게?"

"자, 국밥이오."

배추가 아직 푹 삭질 않아서 뻣뻣했으나 그런대로 먹을 만하였다. 정 씨가 국물을 허겁지겁 퍼 넣고 있는 영달이

The fat woman put down the ladle and let out a big sigh. “That bitch!” she spat out.

Yŏng-dal and Chŏng looked up from where they were sitting, close to the stove, almost hugging it.

“She ran away—the barmaid,” said the fat woman as an explanation. “That’s why the fire got started late. The soup ingredients weren’t ready either.” She turned toward the men who were talking excitedly and shouted, “What are you doing, yakety-yak? Go and catch her. She couldn’t have gone far. Drag her here by the hair.”

“That’s not necessary,” said the master of the house timidly. “She will have to catch the train at Wŏlchul. All we need to do is wait at the station.”

“Then get your bike out and go,” said the fat woman.

“The weather is really beastly...” mumbled the husband.

“What are you talking about? That bitch, Paek-hwa, means fifty thousand *wŏn*.”

“It’s Paek-hwa,” butted in one of the young men, “that brought business to this Seoul Restaurant. She made this the thriving business that it is.”

“G.I.s would sell their boots to come here just for her sake.”

에게 말했다.

"작년 겨울에 어디 있었소?"

들고 있던 국그릇을 내려놓고 영달이는,

"언제요?"

하고 나서 작년 겨울이라고 재차 말하자 껄껄 웃기 시작했다.

"좋았지 정말. 대전 있었습니다. 옥자라는 애를 만났었죠. 그땐 공사장에서 별 볼일두 없었구 노임두 실했어요."

"살림을 했군?"

"의리 있는 여자였어요. 애두 하나 가질 뻔했었는데. 지난봄에 내가 실직을 하게 되자, 돈 모으면 모여서 살자구 서울루 식모 자릴 구해서 떠나갔죠. 하지만 우리 같은 떠돌이가 언약 따위를 지킬 수 있나요. 밤에 혼자 자다가 일어나면 그 애 때문에 남은 밤을 꼬박 새우는 적두 있습니다."

정 씨는 흐려진 영달이의 표정을 무심하게 쳐다보다가, 창밖으로 고개를 돌리고는 조용하게 말했다.

"사람이란 곁에서 오랫동안 두고 보지 않으면 저절로 잊게 되는 법이오."

뒤란으로 나갔던 뚱뚱이 여자가 호들갑을 떨면서 돌아

"Oh, is that so?" said the fat woman scornfully. "Nonsense! A pretty face she may have, but what is she but a common whore? It's me who brings in whatever business there is. Lately she has been making excuses not to work, saying she was sick. She wouldn't fetch water, wouldn't cook, wouldn't even receive customers. Six months at Chansaem and she's all washed out. I was thinking of getting a replacement, as soon as I would get my money back. What are you doing, anyway? Go and wait for her at the station."

"All right, all right." The owner of the restaurant winced at the sharp tone of his wife's voice, and said to the men of the village. "Hurry up! I'll buy you drinks when you come back," urged the wife.

All three men went out.

"Wouldn't it be nice," joked Chŏng, "if we had Paek-hwa pour wine for us?"

"It's going to be a big problem with so many young men visiting here in the evening," grumbled the fat woman.

"You ought to have three or four girls here," said Chŏng.

"With too many girls around, it could be more trouble for me," said the fat woman. "One good-

왔다.

"아유 어쩌나…… 눈이 올 것 같애. 하늘에 먹구름이 잔뜩 끼고, 바람이 부는군. 이놈의 두상이 꼴에 도중에서 가다 말고 돌아올 게 분명하지."

정 씨가 뚱뚱보 여자의 계속될 수다를 막았다.

"월출까지는 몇 리요?"

"한 육십 리 돼요."

"뻐스는 있나요?"

"오후에 두 대쯤 있지요. 이년을 따악 잡아갖구 막차루 돌아올 텐데…… 참, 어디까지들 가슈?"

영달이가 말했다.

"바다가 보이는 데까지."

"바다? 멀리 가시는군. 요 큰길루 가실 거유?"

정 씨가 고개를 끄덕이자 여자는 의자에 궁둥이를 붙인 채로 앞으로 다가앉았다.

"부탁 하나 합시다. 가다가 스물두엇쯤 되고 머리는 긴데다 외눈 쌍까풀인 계집년을 만나면 캐어 봐서 좀 잡아오슈. 내 현금으루 딱, 만 원 내리다."

정 씨가 빙그레 웃었다. 영달이가 자신 있다는 듯이 기세 좋게 대답했다.

looking girl is enough. Besides, I can borrow girls anytime I need them. Do you need girls? Shall I get them for you?"

"What are you talking about?" said Chŏng jokingly. "Making a man play with a girl from early morning—do you want to see me carried out as a corpse in the evening? Is that what you want?"

"Here is your boiled rice in soup." The fat woman brought the soup to the table. It wasn't too bad, though the cabbages could have been softer.

"Where were you last winter?" said Chŏng to Yŏng-dal, who was hastily devouring the soup.

"When?" Yŏng-dal asked back, putting down his spoon. As the other man repeated his question, he started laughing and said. "A hell of a good time it was. Yes, sir! At Taejon. There was this girl I met, Ok-ja. I had an easy job, and good pay, too"

"So you shacked up?" Chŏng encouraged him.

"She was a good girl," continued Yŏng-dal. "You could trust her. We almost had a baby. When I lost my job last spring, she had to go to Seoul to become a maid. We promised to each other that we'd come together as soon as we could make some money, but what is a promise to people like us? When I wake up at night, I think about her and

"그럭허슈. 대신에 데려오면 꼭 만 원 내야 합니다."

"암, 내다뿐이오. 예서 하룻밤 푹 묵었다 가시구려."

"좋았어."

그들은 일어났다. 문을 열고 나오는 그들의 뒷덜미에다 대고 여자가 소리쳤다.

"머리가 길구 외눈 쌍꺼풀이에요. 잊지 마슈."

해가 낮은 구름 속에 들어가 있어서 주위는 누런 색안경을 통해서 내다본 것처럼 뿌옇게 보였다. 바람이 읍내의 신작로 한복판에서 회오리 기둥을 곤두세우고 있었다. 그들은 고개를 처박고 신작로를 따라서 올라갔다. 영달이가 담배 한 갑을 샀다. 들판을 스치고 지나가는 바람 소리가 날카롭게 들려왔다.

그들이 마을 외곽의 작은 다리를 건널 적에 성긴 눈발이 날리기 시작하더니 허공에 차츰 흰색이 빽빽해졌다. 한 스무 채 남짓한 작은 마을을 지날 때쯤 해서는 큰 눈송이를 이룬 함박눈이 펑펑 쏟아져 내려왔다. 눈이 찰지어서 걷기에는 그리 불편하지 않았고 눈보라도 포근한 듯이 느껴졌다. 그들의 모자나 머리카락과 눈썹에 내려앉은 눈 때문에 두 사람은 갑자기 노인으로 변해 버렸다. 도중에 그들은 옛 원님의 송덕비를 세운 비각 앞에서 잠깐 쉬어

can't get back to sleep."

Chŏng calmly looked at Yŏng-dal who almost looked as if he were about to break down. "Out of sight, out of mind, you know. You'll forget," said Chŏng, looking out the window.

The fat woman who had been out in the backyard came back in, complaining. "What a day! It's going to snow. The sky is lowering. The wind is blowing ever so hard. I'm afraid my blockhead of a husband will turn back halfway there."

"How far is it to Wŏlchul?" asked Chŏng, forestalling the fat woman's volley of words, which were likely to become very tiresome.

"About sixty *li*."

"Are there any buses that go there?" Chŏng continued his query.

"Usually there are two buses in the afternoon," answered the woman. "They should be able to catch her and come back by the last bus. By the way, where are you headed?"

"As far as the coast," answered Yŏng-dal.

"That's pretty far. Are you taking the big road?" As Chŏng nodded to the woman's question, she pulled up her chair closer to the two men and continued. "Would you do me a favor? If you come across this

가기로 했다. 그 앞에서 신작로가 두 갈래로 갈라져 있었던 것이다. 함석판에 페인트로 쓴 이정표가 있긴 했으나, 녹이 슬고 벗겨져 잘 알아볼 수도 없었다. 그들은 비각 처마 밑에 웅크리고 앉아서 담배를 피웠다. 정 씨가 하늘을 올려다보며 감탄했다.

"야, 그놈의 눈송이 탐스럽기두 하다. 풍년 들겠어."

"눈 오는 모양을 보니, 근심걱정이 싹 없어지는데……."

"첨엔 기분두 괜찮았지만, 이렇게 오다가는 길 가기가 그리 쉽지 않겠는걸."

"까짓 가는 데까지 가구 내일 또 갑시다. 저기 누가 오는군."

흰 두루마기를 입고 중절모를 깊숙이 내려 쓴 노인이 조심스럽게 걸어오고 있었다. 노인의 모자챙과 접힌 부분 위에 눈이 빙수처럼 쌓여 있었다. 정 씨가 일어나 꾸벅하면서,

"영감님, 길 좀 묻겠습니다요."

"물으슈."

"월출 가는 길이 아랩니까, 저 윗길입니까?"

"윗길이긴 하지만…… 재가 있어 놔서 아무래두 수월친

girl on the road—she is about twenty years old, long hair, double-lidded on one eye—throw some questions to see if she is Paek-hwa and, if she is, bring her back to me. I will give you ten thousand *wŏn* in cash."

Chŏng merely smiled but Yŏng-dal was excited and said confidantly. "Sure. We'll do that. But you must really give us the money you promise now."

"You can depend on me," the woman assured him. "Also, you could stay here overnight."

"Good," said Yŏng-dal.

He rose with Chŏng and walked out of the restaurant. The woman was shouting towards their back, "Long hair, double-lided on one eye. Don't forget."

The sun was hiding behind the low cast clouds. The whole world appeared as if seen through yellow-tinted glasses. The wind formed a column of whirling dust on the main street of the village. Chŏng and Yŏng-dal lowered their heads into their collars and walked up the main street. Yŏng-dal stopped to buy cigarettes. The wind coming across the fields increased its fury.

When they crossed the bridge just outside the village, snow began to fall, at first a few flakes, and

않을 거야. 아마 교통도 두절된 모양인데."

"아랫길은요?"

"거긴 월출 쪽은 아니지만 고을 셋을 지나면, 감천이라구 나오지."

영달이가 물었다.

"감천에 철도가 닿습니까?"

"닿다마다."

"그럼 감천으루 가야겠구만."

정 씨가 인사를 하자 노인은 눈이 가득 쌓인 모자를 위로 들어 보였다. 노인은 윗길 쪽으로 가다가 마을을 향해 꺾어졌다. 영달이는 비각 처마 끝에 회색으로 퇴색한 채 매어져 있는 새끼줄을 끊어 냈다. 그가 반으로 끊은 새끼줄을 정 씨에게도 권했다.

"감발 치구 갑시다."

"견뎌 날까."

새끼줄로 감발을 친 두 사람은 걸음에 한결 자신이 갔다. 그들은 아랫길로 접어들었다. 길은 차츰 좁아졌으나, 소달구지 한 대쯤 지날 만한 길은 그런대로 계속되었다. 길옆은 개천과 자갈밭이었고 눈이 한 꺼풀 덮여 있었다. 뒤를 돌아보면, 길 위에 두 사람의 발자국이 줄기차게 따

then the white stuff filled the whole sky. When they passed through another small village of twenty houses or so, snow fell thick and heavy. It did not make the going any harder, however. On the contrary, the snow blanketed them with a soft downy feeling. It snowed on their hats and hair, turning them into old men. They decided to take a rest in front of a little pavilion, memorial for a country magistrate of old. There the road forked into two. A tin signboard standing by the road indicated distances, but the rust and the paint peeling off made them hard to decipher. Chŏng and Yŏng-dal sat down in front of the pavilion and started smoking.

"Pretty, aren't they? The snowflakes," said Chŏng, looking up at the sky. "The harvest will be good next year."

"When you look at it, you feel as if there is nothing to worry about in the whole world," said Yŏng-dal.

"Yeah, it makes me feel good, too," said Chŏng, "but if it keeps on snowing like this, we will have a difficult time on the road."

"Let's go just as far as we feel like going," proposed Yŏng-dal. "We can continue tomorrow. What's the

라왔다.

마을 하나를 지났다. 그들은 눈 위로 이리저리 뛰어다니는 아이들과 개들 사이로 지나갔다. 마을의 가게 유리창마다 성에가 두껍게 덮여 있었고 창 너머로 사람들의 목소리가 들려왔다. 두 번째 마을을 지날 때엔 눈발이 차츰 걷혀 갔다. 그들은 노변의 구멍가게에서 소주 한 병을 깠다. 속이 화끈거렸다.

털썩, 눈 떨어지는 소리만이 가끔씩 들리는 송림 사이를 지나는데, 뒤에 처져서 걷던 영달이가 주춤 서면서 말했다.

"저것 좀 보슈."

"뭘 말요?"

"저쪽 소나무 아래."

쭈그려 앉은 여자의 등이 보였다. 붉은 코트 자락을 위로 쳐들고 쭈그린 꼴이 아마도 소변이 급해서 외진 곳을 찾은 모양이다. 여자가 허연 궁둥이를 쳐들고 속곳을 올리다가 뒤를 힐끗 돌아보았다.

"오머머!"

여자가 재빨리 코트 자락을 내리고 보퉁이를 집어 들면서 투덜거렸다.

hurry? Look, there's somebody coming this way."

An aged-looking man in a traditional Korean men's white overcoat with a felt hat on his head was walking in their direction, taking care that he should not slip on the snow-covered road. The snow had turned into ice on the brim and the fold of his hat.

"Excuse me, sir," Chŏng said to the old man, bowing low. "Could you tell me which road we should take to Wŏlchul?"

"Certainly. This road goes to Wŏlchul," answered the old man, pointing out the road, "but it won't be easy. There is a steep mountain path you will have to cross. In this snow, I don't think any buses will be going that way."

"Where does the other road lead to?" asked Chŏng.

"Not to Wŏlchul," answered the old man. "After you pass three villages, you'll get to Kamchŏn."

"Does the train go there?" Yŏng-dal asked this time.

"Yes, it does," said the old man.

"Thank you. Let's go." Chŏng said. The old man lifted his snow-covered hat and took to the upper road and soon turned toward the direction of the

"개새끼들 뭘 보구 지랄야."

영달이가 낄낄 웃었고, 정 씨가 낮게 소곤거렸다.

"외눈 쌍꺼풀인데그래."

"어쩐지 예감이 이상하더라니……."

여자는 어딘가 불안했는지 그들에게로 다가오기를 꺼리며 주춤주춤했다. 영달이가 말했다.

"잘 만났는데 백화 아가씨, 찬샘에서 빵소니치는 길이구만."

"무슨 상관야, 내 발루 내가 가는데."

"주인아줌마가 댁을 만나면 잡아다 달래던데."

여자가 태연하게 그들에게로 걸어 나왔다.

"잡아가 보시지."

백화의 얼굴은 화장을 하지 않았는데도 먼 길을 걷느라고 발갛게 달아 있었다. 정 씨가 말했다.

"그런 게 아니라…… 행선지가 어디요? 이 친구 말은 농담이구."

여자는 소변보다가 남자들 눈에 띈 일보다는 영달이의 거친 말솜씨에 몹시 토라져 있었다. 백화가 걸음을 빨리하며 내쏘았다.

"제 따위들이 뭐라구 잡아가구 말구야. 뜨내기 주제

village. Yŏng-dal cut off a piece of faded straw rope hanging from the roof, and handed half of it to Chŏng, saying: "Tie it around your feet."

"Will it be strong enough?" Chŏng voiced his doubt.

They tied the rope over their shoes. Now the two men could walk with surer treads. They turned into the lower road. It soon became narrower but was wide enough to let an ox-cart pass. A stream with gravel borders ran by the road. There was a thin sheet of snow on the stream. The two men kept on walking, leaving behind their footprints in the snow.

They entered a village, and passed through the village children and dogs which were scampering about in the snow-covered fields. The frost was thick on the windows of the village shops. People were talking behind the windows. They passed another village and the snow began to let up. At a little roadside store they bought a bottle of white rice wine and drank it. They began to feel warmer.

Then they walked through a pine forest. The trees let lumps of snow fall with a thud from time to time. Yŏng-dal who had been falling behind called out, "Look!"

"What?" Chŏng looked back.

에.”

“그래, 우리두 너 같은 뜨내기 신세다. 찬샘에 잡아다 주고 여비라두 뜯어 써야겠어.”

영달이가 여자의 뒤를 바싹 쫓아가며 농담이 아님을 재차 강조했다. 여자가 획 돌아서더니, 믿을 수 없을 만큼 재빠르게 영달이의 앞가슴을 밀어냈다. 영달이는 미처 피할 겨를도 없이 눈 위에 궁둥방아를 찧고 나가떨어졌다. 백화가 한 팔은 보퉁이를 끼고, 다른 쪽은 허리에 척 얹고 서서 영달이를 내려다보았다.

“이거 왜 이래? 나 백화는 이래 봬두 인천 노랑집에다, 대구 자갈마당, 포항 중앙대학, 진해 칠구, 모두 겪은 년이라구. 조용히 시골 읍에서 수양하던 참인데…… 야야, 내 배 위로 남자들 사단 병력이 지나갔어. 국으루 가만있다가 조용한 데 가서 한 코 달라면 몰라두 치사하게 뚱보 돈 먹자구 나한테 공갈 때리면 너 죽구 나 죽는 거야.”

영달이는 입을 벌린 채 일어설 줄을 모르고 백화의 일장연설을 듣고 있었다. 정 씨는 웃음을 참느라고 자꾸만 송림 쪽으로 고개를 돌렸다. 영달이가 멋쩍게 궁둥이를 털면서 일어났다.

“우리두 의리가 있는 사람들이다. 치사하다면, 그런 짓

"Look under the pine tree over there." Where Yŏng-dal was pointing, there sat a woman squatting on the ground with her back turned to them. From the way she was squatting, holding up the tails of her red coat with her hands, she must have been urinating. While they were looking, she stood up, exposing her white buttocks before she pulled up her underwear. Then she looked around and exclaimed, "Oh, my!" She let her coat down and picked up her bundle lying where she had been squatting. "What are you looking at, you bastards?" she shouted.

Yŏng-dal sniggered. Chŏng whispered under his breath. "She has a double eyelid on one eye."

"Yeah. I had a funny hunch that we would see her."

The woman was obviously afraid of something and would not come near them.

"So it is you," said Yŏng-dal loudly, "Miss Paek-hwa, running away from Chansaem."

"What's it to you?" She snapped back, "I'm walking on my own feet."

"Your mistress asked us to catch you and bring you back to her," said Yŏng-dal.

The woman walked towards them with defiance

안 해."

세 사람은 나란히 눈 쌓인 길을 걸었다. 백화가 말했다.

"그럼 반말 놓지 말라구요."

영달이는 입맛을 쩍쩍 다셨고, 정 씨가 물었다.

"어디까지 가오?"

"집에요."

"집이 어딘데……."

"저 남쪽이에요. 떠난 지 한 삼 년 됐어요."

영달이가 말했다.

"애네들은 긴 밤 자다가두 툭하면 내일 당장에라두 집에 갈 것처럼 말해요."

백화는 아까와 같은 적의는 나타내지 않았다. 백화는 귀 옆으로 흘러내리는 머리카락을 자꾸 쓰다듬어 올리면서 피곤한 표정으로 영달이를 찬찬히 바라보았다.

"그래요. 밤마다 내일 아침엔 고향으로 출발하리라 작정하죠. 그런데 마음뿐이지, 몇 년이 흘러요. 막상 작정하고 나서 집을 향해 가 보는 적두 있어요. 나두 꼭 두 번 고향 근처까지 가 봤던 적이 있어요. 한번은 동네 어른을 먼발치서 봤어요. 나 이름이 백화지만, 가명이에요. 본명은…… 아무에게도 가르쳐 주지 않아."

and said "All right, catch me!" Paek-hwa looked flushed even without her make-up from the long walk in the cold.

"Not that we want to do it," placated Chŏng. "Where are you headed for? My friend here was only joking."

The woman was very upset less because she had been caught in the act of urinating than because Yŏng-dal's manner of speech was impudent. She said angrily, "Who do you think you are, trying to catch somebody? You are only good-for-nothing bums."

"Yeah, we are bums. So are you. We want to take you to Chansaem and make some money for travel." Yŏng-dal walked up to the woman, trying to show her that he was not merely joking.

Suddenly Paek-hwa swung around fast and pushed off Yŏng-dal's chest with all her strength. Before he realized it, Yŏng-dal was knocked down onto the snow. Paek-hwa stared down at him, with one hand around her bundle and the other at her waist akimbo.

"What do you want, you son of a bitch?" she shouted. "I have been through the 'Yellow House' at Inch'ŏn, the 'Gravel Yard' at Taegu, the 'College'

정 씨가 말했다.

"서울식당 사람들이 월출역으루 지키러 가던데……."

"이런 일이 한두 번인가요 머. 벌써 그럴 줄 알구 감천 가는 길루 왔지요. 촌놈들이니까 그렇지, 빠른 사람들은 서너 군데 길목을 딱 막아 놓아요. 나 그 사람들께 손해 끼친 거 하나두 없어요. 빚이래야 그치들이 빨아먹은 나머지구요. 아유, 인젠 술하구 밤이라면 지긋지긋해요. 밑이 쭉 빠져 버렸어. 어디 가서 여승이나 됐으면…… 냉수에 목욕재계 백 일이면 나두 백화가 아니라구요, 씨팔."

걸을수록 백화는 말이 많아졌고, 걸음은 자꾸 처졌다. 백화는 여러 도시에서 한창 날리던 시절이 얘기를 늘어놓았다. 여자가 결론지은 얘기는 결국 화류계의 사랑이란 돈 놓고 돈 먹기 외에는 모두 사기라는 것이었다. 그 여자는 자기 보퉁이를 꾹꾹 찌르면서 말했다.

"아저씨네는 뭘 갖구 다녀요? 망치나 톱이겠지 머. 요 속에는 헌 속치마 몇 벌, 빤스, 화장품, 그런 게 들었지요. 속치마 꼴을 보면 내 신세하구 똑같아요. 하두 빨아서 빛이 바래구 재봉실이 나들나들하게 닳아 끊어졌어요."

백화는 이제 겨우 스물두 살이었지만 열여덟에 가출해서, 쓰리게 당한 일이 많기 때문에 삼십이 훨씬 넘은 여자

at Pohang, and the 'Seventh District' at Inch'ŏn, and that is not for nothing. I was just taking some rest in that country house. I have let more than a military division of men pass over my belly. If you stayed nice and quiet, I could give you a piece in some quiet corner. If you think that you can sell me off to that fatso for some snotty pay, however, we'll die together, you and me, before you do that."

Sitting on the ground, with his mouth open, Yŏng-dal listened to her harangue. Chŏng looked into the pine trees, trying hard to keep down his laughter that was about to burst out. Yŏng-dal stood up shamefacedly, and dusted off the snow from his trousers.

"We are men of honor," he said. "We don't do mean things."

The three started walking together on the snow-covered road. As she went along with the men, Paek-hwa said, "If you are men of principle as you say, don't forget your manners when speaking to me."

Yŏng-dal merely clicked his tongue, but Chŏng politely asked, "Where are you headed for?"

"For home," she said gruffly.

"Where is your home?"

처럼 조로해 있었다. 한마디로 관록이 붙은 갈보였다. 백화는 소매가 해진 헌 코트에다 무릎이 튀어나온 바지를 입었고, 물에 불은 오징어처럼 되어 버린 낡은 하이힐을 신고 있었다. 비탈길을 걸을 때, 영달이와 정 씨가 미끄러지지 않도록 양쪽에서 잡아 주어야 했다. 영달이가 투덜거렸다.

"고무신이라두 하나 사 신어야겠어. 댁에 때문에 우리가 형편없이 지체되잖나."

"정 그러시면 두 분이서 먼저 가면 될 거 아네요. 내가 고무신 살 돈이 어딨어?"

"우리두 의리가 있다구 그랬잖어. 산속에다 여자를 떼놓구 갈 수야 없지. 그런데…… 한 푼두 없단 말야?"

백화가 깔깔대며 웃었다.

"여자 밑천이라면 거기만 있으면 됐지, 무슨 돈이 필요해요?"

"저러니 언제 한번 온전한 살림 살겠나 말야!"

"이거 봐요. 댁에 같은 훤출한 내 신랑감들은 제 입에 풀칠두 못해서 떠돌아다니는데, 내가 어떻게 살림을 살겠냐구."

영달이는 백화의 입담을 감당할 수가 없었다. 세 사람은

"South. It's been three years since I left home."

"These girls speak so easy—as if one could just get up and go home, just like that." At Yŏng-dal's sarcastic remark, Paek-hwa did not show the same kind of hostility she had shown before. She smoothed the stray hair back from her temples and looked at Yŏng-dal with an expression of fatigue.

"You're right," said Paek-hwa in a calm voice. "We think every night that we will go home first thing in the morning, but that's only what we think at night." Years go by. There are times we really make up our minds and head home. Twice I almost made my way home. Once I looked at the village elders from afar. People call me Paek-hwa, but, of course, that's not my real name. I never tell my real name to anybody."

"They said at the Seoul Restaurant that they were going to Wŏlchul to catch you at the station," Chŏng informed her.

"Well, this isn't the first time," said Paek-hwa. "I knew that they would go there. That's why I took the road to Kamchŏn and came this way. They're just country hicks. If they were smart, they would have sent the guys on all the roads. But I have done nothing that would hurt anybody. My debt? It is

감천 가는 도중에 있는 마지막 마을로 들어섰다. 마을 어귀의 얼어붙은 개천 위로 물오리들이 종종걸음을 치거나 주위를 선회하고 있었다. 마을의 골목길은 조용했고, 굴뚝에서 매캐한 청솔 연기 냄새가 돌담을 휩싸고 있었는데 나직한 창호지의 들창 안에서는 사람들의 따뜻한 말소리들이 불투명하게 들려왔다. 영달이가 정 씨에게 제의했다.

"허기가 져서 속이 떨려요. 감천엔 어차피 밤에 떨어질 텐데, 여기서 뭣 좀 얻어먹구 갑시다."

"여긴 바닥이 작아 주막이나 가게두 없는 거 같군."

"어디 아무 집이나 찾아가서 사정을 해 보죠."

백화도 두 손을 코트 주머니에 찌르고 간신히 발을 떼면서 말했다.

"온몸이 얼었어요. 밥은 고사하고, 뜨뜻한 아랫목에서 발이나 녹이구 갔으면."

정 씨가 두 사람을 재촉했다.

"얼른 지나가지. 여기서 지체하면 하룻밤 자게 될 테니. 감천엘 가면 하숙두 있구, 우리를 태울 기차두 있단 말요."

그들은 이 적막한 산골 마을을 지나갔다. 눈 덮인 들판 위로 물오리 떼가 내려앉았다가는 날아오르곤 했다. 길가

something extra they'd like to suck out of me after all the blood-sucking they have already done. I am sick and tired of booze and nights. I don't want any more of that. No thanks. My bottom just dropped out of my body. I wish I could become a Buddhist nun. To get up at dawn, take a cold shower and pray for a hundred days, then, I'll be Paek-hwa no more... Damn it!"

They continued walking. Paek-hwa became more and more talkative. When she fell behind, she talked from behind. She talked about the times when she enjoyed her popularity in the cities, but her conclusion was that everything was fraudulent, except money—in her world of barmaids. She jabbed her bundle with her forefinger.

"What do you have in your bundle?" Paek-hwa asked the men. "Don't tell me. I know. Hammers and saws. What do I have in my bundle? A couple of old slips, panties, lipsticks, powder and what not. If you look at these things, you'd know how I am doing—washed out, faded, threadbare, worn out like my old slip."

Paek-hwa was only twenty-two, but acted as if she was over thirty. After leaving home at eighteen, she had known the bitter taste of life. Now she was a

에 퇴락한 초가 한 간이 보였다. 지붕의 한쪽은 허물어져 입을 벌렸고 토담도 반쯤 무너졌다. 누군가가 살다가 먼 곳으로 떠나간 폐가임이 분명했다. 영달이가 폐가 안을 기웃해 보며 말했다.

"저기서 신발이라두 말리구 갑시다."

백화가 먼저 그 집의 눈 쌓인 마당으로 절뚝이며 들어섰다. 안방과 건넌방의 구들장은 모두 주저앉았으나 봉당은 매끈하고 딴딴한 흙바닥이 그런대로 쉬어 가기에 알맞았다. 정 씨도 그들을 따라 처마 밑에 가서 엉거주춤 서 있었다. 영달이는 흙벽 틈에 삐죽이 솟은 나무 막대나 문짝, 선반 등속의 땔 만한 것들을 끌어 모아다가 봉당 가운데 쌓았다. 불을 지피자 오랫동안 말라 있던 나무라 노란 불꽃으로 타올랐다. 불길과 연기가 차츰 커졌다. 정 씨마저도 불가로 다가앉아 젖은 신과 바짓가랑이를 불길 위에 갖다 대고 지그시 눈을 감았다. 불이 생기니까 세 사람 모두가 먼 곳에서 지금 막 집에 도착한 느낌이 들었고, 잠이 왔다. 영달이가 긴 나무를 무릎으로 꺾어 불 위에 얹고, 눈물을 흘려 가며 입김을 불어대는 모양을 백화는 이윽히 바라보고 있었다.

"댁에…… 괜찮은 사내야. 나는 아주 치사한 건달인 줄

seasoned prostitute. She wore an old coat frayed at the elbows, a pair of baggy pants, and high-heeled shoes as shapeless as swollen squids. The two men had to give her support when they came upon steep slopes, lest she should slip.

"You could have easily bought yourself a pair of rubber shoes," complained Yŏng-dal. "You are slowing us down."

"If that's the way you feel," she retorted, "why don't you guys go ahead? Where do I get the money to buy the rubber shoes with?"

"Didn't we tell you that we are men of honor?" said Yŏng-dal defensively. "We can't leave a woman alone in the mountains. So you haven't got any money, eh?"

Paek-hwa chuckled. "What does a woman need—if only she has a pussy?

"The way you think, it's no wonder that you have never settled down," jeered Yŏng-dal.

"Look here," Paek-hwa retorted. "What do you think you are yourself? How can a girl like me be a housewife when you handsome guys can't earn enough to feed yourself, let alone a family?"

Yŏng-dal was no match for the barrage of Paek-hwa's sharp answers. Then they came into the last

알았어.”

“이거 왜 이래. 괜히 나이롱 비행기 태우지 말어.”

“아녜요. 불 때는 꼴이 제법 그럴듯해서 그래요.”

정 씨가 싱글벙글 웃으면서 영달에게 말했다.

“저런 무딘 사람 같으니. 이 아가씨가 자네한테 반했다…… 그 말이야.”

“괜히 그러지 마슈. 나두 과거에 연애해 봤소. 계집년이란 사내가 쐬빠지게 해 줘두 쪼끔 벌릴까 말까 한단 말입니다. 이튿날 해만 뜨면 말짱 헛것이지.”

“오머머, 어디 가서 하루살이 연애만 해본 모양이네. 여보세요, 화류계 연애가 아무리 돈에 운다지만 한번 붙으면 순정이 무서운 거예요. 내가 처음 이 길 들어서서 독하게 사랑해 본 적두 있었어요.”

지붕 위의 눈이 녹아서 투덕투덕 마당 위에 떨어지기 시작했다. 여자는 나무막대기를 불 속에 넣고 휘저으면서 갑자기 새촘한 얼굴이 되었다. 불길에 비친 백화의 얼굴은 제법 고왔다.

“그런데…… 몇 명이었는지 알아요? 여덟 명이었어요.”

“진짜 화류계 연애로구만.”

“들어 봐요. 사실은 그 여덟 사람이 모두 한 사람이나

village before the railway station at Kamchŏn. There were wild ducks on the frozen river, tottering with short quick steps or circling around. As the three walked into the village, everything was quiet. There was the stinging smell of burning pine wood, from the chimneys, encircling fences. The blurred murmur of the villagers talking behind the paper windows vaguely spilled over into the streets.

"I feel shaky," confessed Yŏng-dal, "because I haven't eaten anything yet. By the time we get to Kamchŏn, it will be night. Let's get something to eat here."

"This place is too small," objected Chŏng. "There doesn't seem to be any eating places or stores here."

"We could always drop into a house and explain our situation," suggested Yŏng-dal.

Paek-hwa had her hands in the pockets of her coat. She found it difficult to walk on the slippery road. "I'm frozen stiff," she said weakly. "I would like to warm my feet a little bit, even if we don't have anything to eat."

But Chŏng insisted on keeping on the road. "It's better to go on. If we stop here, it means losing one whole night. There are eating places in Kamchŏn. And the train, don't forget that."

마찬가지였거든요."

백화는 주점 '갈매기집'에서의 나날을 생각했다. 그 여자는 날마다 툇마루에 걸터앉아서 철조망의 네 귀퉁이에 높다란 망루가 서 있는 군대 감옥을 올려다보았던 것이다. 언덕 위에 흰 페인트로 칠한 반달형 퀀셋 막사와 바라크가 늘어서 있었고 주위에 코스모스가 만발해 있어, 그 안에 철창이 있고 죄지은 사람들이 하루 종일 무릎을 꿇고 있으리라고는 믿어지질 않았다. 하루에 한 번씩, 긴 구령 소리에 맞춰서 붉은 줄을 친 군복에 박박 깎인 머리의 군 죄수들이 바깥으로 몰려나왔다. 죄수들이 일렬로 서서 세면과 용변을 보는 모습이 보였다. 그들은 간혹 대여섯 명씩 무장 헌병의 감시를 받으며 마을로 작업을 하러 내려오는 때도 있었다. 등에 커다란 광주리를 메고 고개를 숙인 채로 그들은 줄을 지어 걸어왔다.

"처음에 부산에서 잘못 소개를 받아 술집으로 팔렸었지요. 거기에 갔을 땐 벌써 될 대루 되라는 식이어서 겁나는 것두 없었구요, 나이는 어렸지만 인생살이가 고달프다는 것두 깨달았단 말예요."

어느 날 그들은 마을의 제방 공사를 돕기 위해서 삼십여 명이 내려왔다. 출감이 멀지 않은 사람들이라 성깔도

At Chŏng's urging, they kept on walking past the village. Wild ducks would alight on the snowy fields to flutter up again. They found a deserted farm house by the roadside. One corner of the roof had caved in, leaving a gaping hole there, and the dirt wall around the yard was falling into ruins. The farmer and his family must have departed for some other place. Yŏng-dal, who had first looked into the house, said, "Let's go in. We could dry out our shoes here."

Paek-hwa limped into the snow-covered yard, accompanied by the two men. The floors in the inner and the outer rooms had collapsed but the earth floor between the two rooms was still keeping its tamped hardness. It promised to be a place of some comfort and rest. Chŏng walked in last and stood about under the eaves. Yŏng-dal gathered twigs sticking out from under the mud walls, broken doors, shelves—anything that could be burned. They piled the wood in the middle of the earth floor and lit it. The wood that had long dried in the farm house blazed up in orange flames. As the fire and smoke grew, Chŏng, who had been keeping back a little, moved closer, trying to keep his wet shoes and trousers steadily in front of the

부리지 않았고, 마을 사람들도 그리 경원하지 않았다. 그들이 밖으로 작업을 나오면 기를 쓰고 찾는 것은 물론 담배였다. 백화는 담배 두 갑을 사서 그들 중의 얼굴이 해사한 죄수에게 쥐어 주었다. 작업하는 열흘간 백화는 그들의 담배를 댔다. 날마다 그 어려 뵈는 죄수의 손에 몰래 쥐어 주곤 했다. 다음부터 백화는 음식을 장만해서 감옥 면회실로 그를 만나러 갔다. 옥바라지 두 달 만에 그는 이등병 계급장을 달고 백화를 만나러 왔다. 하룻밤을 같이 보내고 병사는 전속지로 떠나갔다.

"그런 식으로 여덟 사람을 옥바라지했어요. 한 달, 두 달, 하다 보면 그이는 앞사람들처럼 하룻밤을 지내구 떠나가군 했어요."

백화는 그런 일 때문에 갈매기집에 있던 시절, 옷 한 가지도 못 해 입었다. 백화는 지나간 삭막한 삼 년 중에서 그때만큼 즐겁고 마음이 평화로웠던 시절은 없었다. 그 여자는 새로운 병사를 먼 전속지로 떠나보내는 아침마다 차부로 나가서 먼지 속에 버스가 가리울 때까지 서 있곤 했었다. 백화는 그 뒤부터 부대 근처를 전전하며 여러 고장을 흘러 다녔다.

아직 초저녁이 분명한데 날씨가 나빠서인지 곧 어두워

fire. He gently closed his eyes. The fire created for them an illusion of having returned home from a long journey. They grew drowsy. Paek-hwa looked on while Yŏng-dal broke twigs over his legs and fed them into the fire, with eyes made teary because of the smoke.

"You're a good man," she said. "I thought you were a mean, rotten egg."

"Why this sudden sweet talk?" Yŏng-dal joked. "Don't be nice now and then put me down."

"Honest," she protested. "I like the way you made the fire."

Chŏng chuckled and said to Yŏng-dal, "You idiot! Can't you see that she fancies you?"

"Don't make fun of me," said Yŏng-dal. "Do you think that I've never been in love? You play all the tricks you know but women barely open up. When the morning comes, they don't care a bit."

"Oh, is that so?" broke in Paek-hwa. "Perhaps you've known only the wrong kinds, fly-by-night loves. They say that, in this whoring world, everything is money, but, once they really fall in love, they really love a formidable love. When I first entered this world, I too had had a life-and-death love."

질 것 같았다. 눈은 더욱 새하얗게 돋보였고, 사위는 고요한데 나무 타는 소리만이 들려왔다.

"감옥뿐 아니라, 세상이란 게 따지면 고해 아닌가……."

정 씨는 벗어서 불가에다 쬐고 있던 잠바를 입으면서 중얼거렸다.

"어둡기 전에 어서 가야지."

그들은 일어났다. 아직도 불길 좋게 타고 있는 모닥불 위에 눈을 한 움큼씩 덮었다. 산천이 차츰 희미하게 어두워졌다. 새들이 이리저리로 깃을 찾아 숲에 모여들고 있었다. 영달이가 백화에게 물었다.

"그래 이젠 어떡할 셈요, 집에 가면……?"

백화가 대답을 않고 웃기만 했다. 정 씨가 말했다.

"시집가야지 뭐."

"시집은 안 가요. 이제 와서 무슨 시집이에요. 조용히 틀어박혀 집의 농사나 거들지요. 동생들이 많아요."

사방이 어두워지자 그들도 얘기를 그쳤다. 어디에나 눈이 덮여 있어서 길을 잘 분간할 수가 없었다. 뒤에 처졌던 백화가 눈 덮인 길의 고랑에 빠져 버렸다. 발이라도 삐었는지 백화는 꼼짝 못하고 주저앉아 신음을 했다. 영달이가 달려들어 싫다고 뿌리치는 백화를 업었다. 백화는 영

The snow melting on the roof fell onto the yard and made a soft dull thud. Paek-hwa poked the fire with a stick and fell into deep thought. Her face, lit by the fire, looked pretty.

"How many men have I loved like that?" she continued. "Eight—eight altogether."

"Just like the way it is in your world," said Yŏng-dal scornfully.

"Listen, all eight of them were like one man to me." Paek-hwa's memory ran back to her life at the Gull House. She used to sit at the tip of the veranda and look toward the military prison with watch-towers at the four corners of the barbed wire fence. On the hill, there was a white-washed crescent quonset hut and several barracks. There were cosmos flowers all around. It was hard to believe that prisoners were actually inside kneeling all day long behind the iron bars. Once a day the prisoners with closely shaven heads and red-striped fatigues marched out of the barracks in regular military formation as the order was given in a long, sharp voice. They washed their faces and defecated—standing or sitting all in single file. Sometimes they came down to the village by fives or sixes led by the armed military police to work around the

달이의 등에 업히면서 말했다.

"무겁죠?"

영달이는 대꾸하지 않았다. 백화가 어린애처럼 가벼웠다. 등이 불편하지도 않았고 어쩐지 가뿐한 느낌이었다. 아마 쇠약해진 탓이리라 생각하니 영달이는 어쩐지 대전에서의 옥자가 생각나서 눈시울이 화끈했다. 백화가 말했다.

"어깨가 참 넓으네요. 한 세 사람쯤 업겠어."

"댁이 근수가 모자라니 그렇다구."

그들은 일곱 시쯤에 감천 읍내에 도착했다. 마침 장이 섰었는지 파장된 뒤인데도 읍내 중앙은 흥청대고 있었다. 전 부치는 냄새, 고기 굽는 냄새, 곰국 냄새가 풍겨 왔다. 영달이는 이제 백화를 옆에서 부축하고 있었다. 발을 디딜 때마다 여자가 얼굴을 찡그렸다. 정 씨가 백화에게 물었다.

"어느 방향이오?"

"전라선이에요."

"나는 호남선 쪽인데. 여비는 있소?"

"군용차를 사정해서 타구 가면 돼요."

그들은 장터 모퉁이에서 아직도 따뜻한 온기가 남아 있는 팥 시루떡을 사 먹었다. 백화가 자기 몫에서 절반을 떼

village. When they did, they marched in orderly columns, keeping their heads down, with oversize baskets slung over their shoulders.

"It all began when I was unlucky enough to run into a man and be sold to a saloon," Paek-hwa reminisced. "When I first walked in there, I didn't care what became of me. I wasn't afraid of anything. I was young, but I knew already how tough life could be."

One day thirty prisoners came to the village to work on the dyke. They were a quiet sort, having come almost to the end of their prison terms. To these prisoners, the villagers lowered their guard a little. Once the prisoners were out in the village, what they wanted most was cigarettes. Once I bought two packs of cigarettes and quietly gave them to a pale-looking prisoner. Then, when they worked in the village, I would supply them regularly with cigarettes through the pale-faced soldier. It then developed that I went to see him at the prison with a present of food. After two months he got out of prison and came to see me. He had the insignia of a private on his fatigues. We spent the night together and he went away to his new post.

어 영달에게 내밀었다.

"더 드세요. 날 업구 왔으니 기운이 배나 들었을 텐데."

역으로 가면서 백화가 말했다.

"어차피 갈 곳이 정해지지 않았다면 우리 고향에 함께 가요. 내 일자리를 주선해 드릴께."

"내야 삼포루 가는 길이지만, 그렇게 하지?"

정 씨도 영달이에게 권유했다. 영달이는 흙이 덕지덕지 달라붙은 신발 끝을 내려다보며 아무 말이 없었다. 대합실에서 정 씨가 영달이를 한쪽으로 끌고 가서 속삭였다.

"여비 있소?"

"빠듯이 됩니다. 비상금이 한 천 원쯤 있으니까."

"어디루 가려우?"

"일자리 있는 데면 어디든지……."

스피커에서 안내하는 소리가 웅얼대고 있었다. 정 씨는 대합실 나무 의자에 피곤하게 기대어 앉은 백화 쪽을 힐끗 보고 나서 말했다.

"같이 가시지. 내 보기엔 좋은 여자 같군."

"그런 거 같아요."

"또 알우? 인연이 닿아서 말뚝 박구 살게 될지. 이런 때 아주 뜨내기 신셀 청산해야지."

"I worked for eight soldiers like that," Paek-hwa continued. "After a month or two, they came out and spent a night with me and went away."

Because of these things, Paek-hwa could not save enough money at the Gull House to buy herself even a new dress. Nevertheless, that was the time when she felt most happy and at peace. On the morning a new soldier departed for a remote post, she would stand and wait until his bus disappeared into the dust on the road. Ever since the Gull House, Paek-hwa made it a rule to stay near military posts when she had to move about from place to place. She ended her story.

It was still early in the evening, but because of the overcast sky felt like night already. The snow looked even whiter. Everything was completely quiet except the crackling of the fire.

"It's not only prison life that is hard," Chŏng added his observation. "Life is a sea of suffering, as they say." He put on his jacket he had been drying over the fire. "Let's be on our way before it gets too dark," he said.

They all stood up and went out to carry in snow by the handfuls to smother the fire that was still burning vigorously. The scenery was gradually

영달이는 시무룩해져서 역사 밖을 멍하니 내다보았다. 백화는 뭔가 쑤군대고 있는 두 사내를 불안한 듯이 지켜보고 있었다. 영달이가 말했다.

"어디 능력이 있어야죠."

"삼포엘 같이 가실라우?"

"어쨌든……."

영달이가 뒷주머니에서 꼬깃꼬깃한 오백 원짜리 두 장을 꺼냈다.

"저 여잘 보냅시다."

영달이는 표를 사고 삼립빵 두 개와 찐 달걀을 샀다. 백화에게 그는 말했다.

"우린 뒤차를 탈 텐데…… 잘 가슈."

영달이가 내민 것들을 받아 쥔 백화의 눈이 붉게 충혈되었다. 그 여자는 더듬거리며 물었다.

"아무도…… 안 가나요?"

"우린 삼포루 갑니다. 거긴 내 고향이오."

영달이 대신 정 씨가 말했다. 사람들이 개찰구로 나가고 있었다. 백화가 보퉁이를 들고 일어섰다.

"정말, 잊어버리지…… 않을게요."

백화는 개찰구로 가다가 다시 돌아왔다. 돌아온 백화는

fading into darkness. Birds were flocking into the woods, homing to their nests there.

"What are your plans after you get home?" Yŏng-dal asked Paek-hwa. She merely laughed and did not answer. Chŏng said in her place, "She will get married."

"No, I am not going to be married," retorted Paek-hwa. "No, sir. I will merely stay at home and help with the fields. Besides, I have many brothers to take care of."

As darkness set in, the three travellers fell into silence. Snow was everywhere, and it was difficult to know where the road lay. Paek-hwa, who had fallen behind the others, stumbled into a ditch. She fell and groaned, not moving. She might have sprained her ankle. Yŏng-dal walked back and, over her protest, took her on his back. Paek-hwa yielding to Yŏng-dal's insistence, said, "Heavy, eh?"

Yŏng-dal did not answer but he thought that she was as light as a child. Far from feeling weighed down with the burden, he felt more light-footed. Maybe she wasn't well. As Yŏng-dal thought about it, he remembered Ok-ja at Taejon and sadness came upon his heart.

"You have broad shoulders," complimented Paek-

눈이 젖은 채 웃고 있었다.

"내 이름 백화가 아니에요. 본명은요…… 이점례예요."

여자는 개찰구로 뛰어나갔다. 잠시 후에 기차가 떠났다.

그들은 나무 의자에 기대어 한 시간쯤 잤다. 깨어 보니 대합실 바깥에 다시 눈발이 흩날리고 있었다. 기차는 연착이었다. 밤차를 타려는 시골 사람들이 의자마다 가득 차 있었다. 두 사람은 말없이 담배를 나눠 피웠다. 먼 길을 걷고 나서 잠깐 눈을 붙였더니 더욱 피로해졌던 것이다. 영달이가 혼잣말로,

"쳇, 며칠이나 견디나……."

"뭐라구?"

"아뇨, 백화란 여자 말요. 저런 애들…… 한 사날두 촌 생활 못 배겨 나요."

"사람 나름이지만 하긴 그럴 거요. 요즘 세상에 일이 년 안으루 인정이 휙 변해 가는 판인데……."

정 씨 옆에 앉았던 노인이 두 사람의 행색과 무릎 위의 배낭을 눈 여겨 살피더니 말을 걸어왔다.

"어디 일들 가슈?"

"아뇨, 고향에 갑니다."

"고향이 어딘데……."

hwa. "You could easily carry three persons at a time."

"It's because you are so underweight," said Yŏng-dal.

It was around seven o'clock when they arrived at Kamchŏn. It must have been the market day. One could still feel the bustle even after the market was closed. Aromas of fried fish, roasted meat, and tripe soup were floating in the air. Yŏng-dal now walked along with Paek-hwa, supporting her from the side. Every step she took made her groan from pain.

"What line are you taking?" Chŏng asked Paek-hwa.

"The Chŏlla Line."

"I'm taking the Honam Line," explained Chŏng. "Do you have enough money for the fare?"

"I could ask soldiers on the military train to give me a free ride," answered Paek-hwa.

At a store in the marketplace they bought several rice cakes and shared them. They were still warm from the steam cooker. Paek-hwa offered half of her share to Yŏng-dal, saying, "You'd better take it. You need that for having carried me on your back."

On the way to the railway station Paek-hwa turned again to Yŏng-dal and suggested, "If you

"삼포라구 아십니까?"

"어 알지, 우리 아들놈이 거기서 도자를 끄는데……."

"삼포에서요? 거 어디 공사 벌릴 데나 됩니까? 고작해야 고기잡이나 하구 감자나 매는데요."

"어허! 몇 년 만에 가는 거요?"

"십 년."

노인은 그렇겠다며 고개를 끄덕였다.

"말두 말우, 거긴 지금 육지야. 바다에 방둑을 쌓아 놓구, 추럭이 수십 대씩 돌을 실어 나른다구."

"뭣 땜에요?"

"낸들 아나. 뭐 관광호텔을 여러 채 짓는담서, 복잡하기가 말할 수 없데."

"동네는 그대루 있을까요?"

"그대루가 뭐요. 맨 천지에 공사판 사람들에다 장까지 들어섰는걸."

"그럼 나룻배두 없어졌겠네요."

"바다 위로 신작로가 났는데, 나룻배는 뭐에 쓰오. 허허 사람이 많아지니 변고지. 사람이 많아지면 하늘을 잊는 법이거든."

작정하고 벼르다가 찾아가는 고향이었으나, 정 씨에게

don't have any particular place you are going to, why don't you come along with me to my village? I can get you work easy enough."

"Sampo is where I am going, but there's no reason why you can't go with her," said Chŏng to Yŏng-dal.

Yŏng-dal looked down at the tips of his clay-covered shoes and didn't say anything.

When they were inside the station, Chŏng took Yŏng-dal aside and asked, "Do you have the fare?"

"Just enough," answered Yŏng-dal. "I have with me a little that I have been setting aside for emergencies. About a thousand *wŏn*."

"Where do you want to go?" asked Chŏng.

"Wherever there is work..."

Arrivals and departures were being announced through the speakers. Chŏng looked at Paek-hwa seated tiredly on a wooden bench in the waiting room, and then said to Yŏng-dal. "Why don't you go with her? She looks like a good girl."

"I think so, too," agreed Yŏng-dal.

"You never know," continued Chŏng. "If things go well, you may be settling down with her. This seems like a good chance for trying."

Yŏng-dal looked outside uncertainly. Paek-hwa stared with an anxious look at the two men talking

는 풍문마저 낯설었다. 옆에서 잠자코 듣고 있던 영달이가 말했다.

“잘됐군. 우리 거기서 공사판 일이나 잡읍시다.”

그때에 기차가 도착했다. 정 씨는 발걸음이 내키질 않았다. 그는 마음의 정처를 잃어 버렸던 때문이었다. 어느결에 정 씨는 영달이와 똑같은 입장이 되어 버렸다.

기차가 눈발이 날리는 어두운 들판을 향해서 달려갔다.

『삼포 가는 길』, 창비, 2000(1973)

under their breath.

"I don't have anything to settle down with," said Yŏng-dal after a moment.

"Then, do you still want to come to Sampo with me?"

"In any case," said Yŏng-dal, producing out of the back pocket of his pants two five-hundred-wŏn bills rolled up tight. "Let's send her on."

Yŏng-dal bought a ticket, two rolls of bread and a hard-boiled egg and walked up to Paek-hwa. "We'll take a later train. So, goodbye now."

Paek-hwa took what Yŏng-dal gave her. Tearing up, she stuttered, "You... are you not going, either of you?"

"We are going to Sampo, that is my home town," answered Chŏng on behalf of them both.

People were going out to the ticket gate. Paek-hwa got up with the bundle under her arm.

"I won't forget your kindness," she said, and walked towards the gate. But then she turned around and came back. Tears stil in her eyes, she was smiling, "My real name is," she said to the two men standing, "not Paek-hwa but Jŏmrye, Yi Jŏmrye. I wanted to tell you that."

She left for the ticket gate once again. And shortly

thereafter the train left the station.

The two men fell asleep on the bench. When they woke up again, about an hour later, it was snowing outside. Their train was late. All the benches in the waiting room were filled with people from the area. They were all waiting for the night trains. The two men lit cigarettes and sat smoking. A short sleep after a long walk made them feel even more exhausted.

"How many days would it last?" said Yŏng-dal as if to himself.

"What do you mean?" Chŏng sat up.

"Her determination to stay and work on the farm. Those kids, they can't stand the farm more than three days."

"Depends on what kind of a person she is. But you are right. People are becoming funny these days."

An old man who had been sitting next to them, looking them over along with their bundles, spoke to them. "Where are you headed?"

"Home," said Chŏng.

"Where is that?" asked the old man.

"Sampo. Have you ever heard of it?"

"Sure," said the old man. "My son works there. He

is a bulldozer operator."

"At Sampo? A bulldozer operator?" said Chŏng incredulously. "There can't be any big time construction work there. Some fishing and potato farming, that's all they have."

"Oh?" the old man exclaimed. "How long have you been away?"

"Ten years," answered Chŏng.

The old man nodded his head. "So you don't know anything. Sampo is now part of the mainland. They built a dyke into the sea. And along the dyke, trucks are carrying tons and tons of rocks and gravel and dumping them into the sea."

"Why?" asked Chŏng.

"Who knows? They say they're going to build some tourist hotels. Who'd know the racket behind all that?"

"I suppose the village hasn't changed, though," said Chŏng hopefully.

"What do you mean? The whole place is full of construction workers. They even have a marketplace there."

"Then, there is now no ferry boat to Sampo?"

"What is the use of any boat?" the old man continued to tell him. "There's a road right over the sea. The problem is people, so many people crowded into one small place. Crowds do away with the old ways of Heaven."

It was a decision made with a strong determination—Chŏng going back home, but the old man's story was something entirely unexpected. He hadn't taken into account the change occurring in his own home town. Yŏng-dal had been listening in silence. Then he said, "Well, that's all the better. We will get work at the construction sites."

As Yŏng-dal was talking, the train came in. Chŏng did not feel like going. He had just lost his heart's home. Now he was in the same situation as Yŏng-dal.

The train pulled out into the dark plain where snow was falling.

Translated by Kim U-chang

해설

Afterword

완벽한 구성과 탁월한 상징

방현석(소설가)

황석영은 이미 한국문학사의 중요한 일부가 되었다.

그는 고등학교 시절에 당시 한국에서 가장 영향력 있는 잡지였던 《사상계》의 신인문학상에 입선, 화제를 불러일으켰다. 한동안 문단에서 사라졌던 황석영이 다시 작품활동을 시작한 것은 팔 년 뒤인 1970년이었다. 그사이 그는 다니던 대학을 중퇴하고 떠돌이 노동자들과 어울려 방랑하다 해병대에 입대했다.

그의 부대는 미국 정부의 요청을 받은 한국 정부의 결정에 따라 베트남전쟁에 투입되었다. 황석영은 베트남에서 강대국 중심의 세계 질서가 불러일으키는 참극을 목격하고, 문학적 대응을 결심한다. 1970년 《조선일보》 신춘

Flawless Structure and Superb Symbolism

Bang Hyun-seok (novelist)

There is no question that Hwang Sok-yong is already an essential part of Korean literary history.

While in high school, he became a sensation by winning the Rookie of the Year Prize from *Sa-sang-gye*, the most influential literary magazine at the time in South Korea. It was in 1970, after eight years of silence, that Hwang Sok-yong returned to the world of creative writing. By then, he had dropped out of college, wandered around with transient laborers, and joined the marines.

At the U.S. government's request, the Korean administration committed his company, along with others, to the Vietnam War. Witnessing firsthand the

문예 소설 부문 당선작인 「탑」은 그 첫 번째 결실이었다.

'탑'을 지키라는 작전 명령을 받은 한국군은 처절하게 싸우며 임무를 수행한다. 그러나 뒤이어 당도한, 작전 계획을 수립한 미군은 그 탑을 탱크로 밀어 버린다. 한국군에게 부여되었던, 목숨을 걸고 지켜야 할 가치는, 그 가치를 부여했던 미군에 의해 한순간에 아무런 가치도 없는 것이 되어 버리고 만다.

황석영이란 이름을 한국문학사에 뚜렷하게 각인시킨 작품은 「객지」와 「삼포 가는 길」이다. 1971년에 발표한 「객지」는 1970년대 한국 사회의 특징을 탁월하게 담아내고 있다. 당시 한국 사회는 농업 중심에서 공업 중심으로 산업 질서가 재편되고 있었다. 급격하게 농촌이 해체되면서 농민들은 일자리를 찾아 고향을 떠났다. 그러나 아직 산업화는 초기 단계에 머물러 있었고, 안정된 일자리를 제공할 공장은 드물었다. 고향을 떠나온 농민들의 대부분은 공사장을 전전하는 떠돌이 노동자가 되었다. 「객지」는 바로 그런 노동자들의 초상이었다.

1973년 발표된 「삼포 가는 길」은 「객지」가 이룬 문학적 성취의 완결판에 해당한다. 이 작품은 길 위의 삶을 다룬 여행 소설의 형식을 가지고 있다. 주인공 영달은 길 위에

tragedies often brought about by a world order centered on the super powers, he decided to challenge that situation with his pen. "The Tower", which took the grand prize for the category of novel in the Annual Open Call for first time writers by the *Choseon Daily* newspaper in 1970 was the first result of this resolve.

Following an order to defend the "Tower" a Korean company goes through a harrowing, costly battle to fulfill their mission, only to see the tower flattened by U.S. army tanks that arrive later on the battlefield, though the operation had been planned by the U.S. military itself. The value the Korean soldiers were charged with risking their lives to defend is discarded as worthless by the American military that established and imposed that value in the first place.

The two pieces that have permanently enshrined Hwang Sok-yong in the pantheon of Korean literature are "Away From Home" and "The Road To Sampo". Published in 1971, "Away From Home" astutely captures the characteristics of Korean society at the time. Around 1970, South Korea was undergoing a reorganization of its economy, moving from an agriculture-centered one to a manufactur-

서 만난 정 씨와 함께 정 씨의 고향인 삼포를 찾아가지만 예전의 삼포는 사라지고 없다. 삼포는 고유명사로서 지명이 아니라 두고 온 고향을 상징하는 추상명사다. 몰려오는 겨울과 함께 공사장은 문을 닫았다. 갈 곳이 없어진 그들은 기억을 더듬어 고향을 찾아갔지만 과거는 이미 해체되고 없다. 과거는 해체되었고, 새로이 발붙일 곳은 없는 서러운 사람들의 운명을 정밀한 필치로 그려 낸 작품이 「삼포 가는 길」이다. 이 소설을 관통하는 건조한 시선 뒤에 불우한 인생에 대한 연민의 눈물이 감춰져 있음을 독자들은 소설을 다 읽은 다음에야 눈치챈다. 「삼포 가는 길」의 미학적 성취는 완벽하게 구축된 장면과 오감을 파고드는 상징체계에서 그 빛을 더한다.

칼바람이 부는 겨울 들판은 잘 만들어진 영화보다도 더 영상적이다. 그리고 그 겨울 들판은 힘과 속도를 숭배하며 국민의 기본권을 차압했던 서슬 퍼런 군사정권에 대한 상징이기도 했다.

「삼포 가는 길」을 쓴 이듬해 황석영은 『장길산』(1984)이라는 대하장편소설의 집필에 뛰어들었다. 권력의 횡포에 맞선 역사 속의 의적을 다룬 이 소설을 무려 십 년 동안 일간지에 연재하면서 황석영은 독자들의 뜨거운 사랑

ing-based one. With farming communities rapidly disintegrating, much of the farming population left their homes in search of work. However, industrialization was still in its infancy, and few factories offered secure employment opportunities. Most uprooted farmers became transient laborers who migrated from one construction site to the next. "Away From Home" was a portrait of such laborers.

Published in 1973, "The Road To Sampo" completes the literary journey that "Away From Home" begins. It is written as a travel diary, logging life on the road. The protagonist, Yŏng-dal, meets Mr. Chŏng, and the two visit Mr. Chŏng's hometown, Sampo, only to find that the old Sampo is no more. Sampo is a proper noun, but it refers to no actual place. Instead it is used as an abstract word symbolizing a hometown that has been left behind. With winter rushing in, the construction site shuts down, and the two have no other place to go to. Relying on fleeting memories, they go searching for this hometown, but the past has dissolved and vanished. "The Road To Sampo" paints in delicate brush-strokes the fate of the wretched, who have neither a past to go back to nor a new reality to get a foothold in. Only at the end of the story does the

을 받는 작가가 되었다.

작가로서 황석영은 문학적 성취와 함께 대중의 사랑을 받는 행운을 누렸다. 그러나 자연인으로서 황석영의 삶에는 많은 시련이 뒤따랐다. 그것은 격변의 현대사를 한국에서 통과한 그의 세대가 감당해야 할 운명이기도 했지만, 그 스스로 말했듯이 '미지의 세상과 새로운 체험에 대한 강렬한 호기심'이 그를 시련의 현장에 데려다 둔 것이기도 했다.

특히 남북이 팽팽하게 대치하고 있는 상황에서 북한을 방문한 결과는 그를 삼 년의 망명과 오 년의 감옥 생활을 감수하게 만들었다. 그러나 그 어떤 난관도 그로부터 작가로서의 직업적 정열을 꺾지는 못했다. 감옥에서 나온 다음에도 그는 무력감에 빠지지 않았다. 엄숙주의에 사로잡히지도 않았다. 오직 작품으로 독자들에게 다시 신임을 물었다. 분단 상황이 지속되고 있는 한반도의 특수성과 21세기 인류의 보편적인 양상으로 부상하고 있는 디아스포라의 문제를 결합시킨 작품 『바리데기』(2007)는 그가 여전히 가장 치열한 현재 진행형 작가임을 입증시켰다.

그는 최근 자신의 트위터에 다음과 같은 글을 올렸다.

"사람은 누구나 낮은 단계의 성취를 이루는 데도 지옥

reader sense the tears of compassion behind the impassive viewpoint sustained throughout. The aesthetic achievement of "The Road To Sampo" shines in its flawlessly constructed scenes and its sensually arousing symbolic system. Winter fields swept by piercing winds are evoked with more visual power than in most well-made films. Furthermore, the winter field serves as an effective symbol of the ruthless military regime that worshipped power and speed while seizing the basic rights of citizens.

The year after publishing "The Road To Sampo", Hwang Sok-yong plunged into writing an epic novel titled *Chang Gil-san* (1984). This story of a Robin Hood in Korean history who stood up to tyrannical power was serialized for no fewer than ten years in a major daily newspaper, earning Hwang the feverish devotion of readers.

As an author, Hwang Sok-yong has enjoyed the good fortune of achieving both artistic triumph and popular admiration. Personally, Hwang has been tested by adversity all his life, a fate he shares with his generation that has had to live through the turbulent modern history of Korea, but he has also been driven to the scenes of trials and tribulations

을 통과하지 않으면 안 된다. 자기 한계점을 넘어서야 하고, 당분간은 그것으로 버티지만, 곧 나태해지기 전에 다시 지옥을 헤쳐 나가야 할 준비를 해야 한다."

그는 이미 한국문학사의 중요한 일부가 되었다. 그러나 더 중요한 것은 그가 여전히 지옥을 헤쳐 나갈 준비를 하고 있다는 사실이다.

by his own intense curiosity about the unknown and his desire for new experiences, as he himself has acknowledged.

In particular, Hwang's trip to North Korea during a period of high tension between North and South cost him three years in exile and five years in prison. None of these challenges, however, frustrated his passion for writing as a consummate professional. Even his years in prison could not make him feel powerless. Nor did he succumb to stoic moralisms. He only wanted his readers to meet and judge him again through his work. He was reaffirmed as the fiercest author on the cutting edge with the publication of *Paridegi* (2007), a synthesis of the particularity of the Korean peninsula's ongoing partition and the universality of diaspora as an emerging phenomenon faced by all of humanity in the 21st century.

Hwang Sok-yong recently twittered the following quote.

"Without exception, you have to go through Hell even for a low level of achievement. You have to overcome your limitations, and then you can go on for a little while, but soon, before complacency sets in, you need to prepare to go through hell again."

Hwang Sok-yong is already an important part of Korean literary history. What's more important, though, is the fact that he is again preparing himself for the next hell.

비평의 목소리

Critical Acclaim

「삼포 가는 길」의 영달과 백화는 시대와 현실을 반영하고 있는 인물이면서도 동시에 시대를 넘어선 차원에서 문학의 영원성이라는 이름의 자리로 격상될 수 있었다. 아울러 작가 황석영이 창조한 인물의 성격에 우리가 몰입하게 되면서 생겨나는 감동의 자장을 우리는 꼭 적어 두어야 한다. 세상의 험난한 길 위에서 어렵게 그러나 진정하게 인간의 길을 발견해 나가는 인물들의 행적이 우리를 감동의 진폭 안에 사로잡히게 한다.

우찬제

그의 이런 둔화되지 않는 현실감각은 어디서 오는 것인

Yŏng-dal and Paek-hwa in "The Road to Sampo" are characters that can represent specific experiences of their times as well as eternal traits of human beings. While reading this story and being drawn into the world of these characters created by Hwang Sok-yong, the master novelist, we cannot help being deeply moved by it. Following these characters on their own way to a hard, but truthful life on the treacherous road of our world, we remain within their sphere of influence.

U Ch'an-je

Where does this sharp insight into reality come

가. 앞서 그가 오 년에 걸친 영어(囹圄) 생활을 겪었다고 했다. 그 영어 생활은 1989년부터 1993년에 이르는 북한, 미국, 독일을 넘나드는 오랜 방랑에서 연유한 것이다. 그의 사십 대 후반과 오십 대 전반을 다 바친 각각 오 년씩의 이 방랑과 투옥, 떠돎과 갇힘의 극적인 경험이 바로 그를 과거의 작가가 아니라 조금의 유보도 없는 '오늘의 작가'로 만들었을 것이다. 그 자신이 아닌 어느 누구도 그 십 년을 다 짐작할 수는 없을 것이다. 다만 그가 여러 차례에 걸친 방북을 통해 달의 저편처럼 이곳에서는 볼 수 없는 분단 체제의 다른 한쪽을 읽었을 것이라는 사실, 현실사회주의의 몰락과 자본주의적 세계 질서의 재편이라는 세계사적 변동이 진행되는 동안 독일과 미국 등의 역사적 현장에 있었다는 사실, 그리고 그것들을 곰삭이고 깁고 추스르는 오 년의 징역 생활 동안 그의 작가적 정체성 속에서 어떤 '의미 있는 것'이 만들어졌으리라는 사실을 짐작할 수 있을 뿐이다.

김명인

황석영은 그동안 우리 문학에서 거의 외면되다시피 해온 막벌이 노동자들을 주인공으로 등장시켜, 모든 사회적

from? I mentioned above that he was imprisoned for about five years. His imprisonment is related to the many years of wanderings throughout North Korea, the US, and Germany from 1989 to 1993. We might be able to say that these years of wandering and imprisonment—five years each—during his late 40's through early 50's made him a "writer of today" rather than a writer of the past. Nobody but himself could presume to know what he had experienced and learned during those ten years. We know, however, that he must have seen the other side of our divided country, invisible to us like the other side of the moon, through his multiple visits to North Korea; that he lived in the US and Germany during the time when the socialist regimes collapsed and the capitalist world order was established; and that he, the writer, must have forged something meaningful out of these experiences during five years of his imprisonment.

Kim Myung-in

Hwang Sok-yong spotlighted the lives of day laborers, which had been almost completely neglected in Korean literature, and warmly and

악조건과 감연히 맞서 싸우는 그들의 생활 현장을 치열한 인간적 공감 속에서 묘사하였다. 이 작품에서 이룩된 가장 감동적인 성과의 하나는 작가가 현실을 묘사함에 있어서 어떤 관념적 도식을 앞세우지 않고 있음에도 불구하고 이 시대의 사회적 현실을 가장 핵심적인 차원에서 제시하고 있다는 사실로 나타난다.

염무웅

sympathetically described their courageous struggle with various adverse social conditions. One of the most moving achievements of this story by Hwang is that it presents the most essential dimension of the social reality of our time without following any fixed ideological formula.

Yom Mu-ung

황석영

작가 황석영(본명 황수영)은 1943년 만주국 신징〔新京〕, 지금의 창춘〔長春〕에서 사 남매 중 막내로 출생했다. 해방을 맞아 창춘에서 무일푼이 된 황석영의 가족은 평양 외가로 갔다가 1947년 다시 38선을 넘어 남한에 정착한다. 전쟁통에 초등학교를 여러 번 옮겼으나 남달리 교육열이 강한 어머니 영향 아래 많은 책을 읽는다. 황석영은 빼어난 글짓기 솜씨로 담임 선생님으로부터 칭찬을 듣고, 전국 어린이 백일장에 나가 1등을 하기도 한다. 유년시절부터 문명을 날리던 황석영은 고교 시절 문예현상공모 세 군데에 입상함으로써 거목의 자질을 드러낸다. 글쓰기에서 재능을 인정받은 황석영은 학교 공부를 게을리하여 낙제를 하고, 급기야 휴학과 자퇴로 바깥을 떠돌다가 가출하여 남도 지방을 방랑하게 된다. 그리고 1962년 11월 단편 「입석부근」을 《사상계》에 투고하여 스무 살이라는 어린 나이로 신인문학상을 수상한다. 암벽 등반 이야기를 다룬 「입석부근」은 고교 등산반 시절 만났던 이들을 모델

Hwang Sok-yong

Hwang Sok-yong (née Hwang Su-yong) was born as the last child among four siblings in Shinjing, Manjukuo (currently Changchun, China) in 1943. After the liberation of Korea, his poverty-stricken family first moved in with his mother's family in Pyong-yang and then moved to South Korea in 1947. As his family moved often during the war, he had to frequently transfer schools, but his education-conscious mother guided him into reading a lot of books. Talented at writing, Hwang received praises from his teachers and won the First Place Award at the National Children's Writing Contest. During high school, he won awards from three different writing competitions, exhibiting his unusual talent. Hwang, however, neglected and failed in schoolwork, and ended up taking a leave of absence, quitting school, and wandering around the southern region of Korea. He made his literary debut in 1962, when he was only twenty, by winning the *Sasang-gye* New Writer Award with his

로 했는데, 황석영은 이들과 함께 '이유 없는 반항기'의 십대 지식인 사회를 형성하여 어울려 다니면서 문학책뿐 아니라 다양한 책들을 섭렵한다.

1964년 대학을 다니던 황석영은 한일 회담 반대 시위에 나섰다가 경찰에 붙잡혀 노량진 경찰서로 끌려가게 되는데, 그곳에서 제2한강교 공사장에서 일하던 한 노동자를 만나고 그를 따라 간척지 공사장, 신탄진 공사장 등을 돌아다닌다. 이때부터 사회의 밑바닥을 떠도는 작가의 본격적인 편력이 시작된 셈이다. 천방지축 저잣거리를 떠돌던 작가는 동래 범어사를 거쳐 금강원에서 다소곳이 행자 노릇을 하다가 어머니에게 덜미가 잡혀 집으로 끌려간다. 그 뒤에도 방랑의 궤적을 벗어나지 못하고 떠돌던 작가는 1966년 해병대에 입대하여 이듬해 청룡부대 제2진으로 베트남전에 참전하게 된다. 베트남에서 황석영은 밑바닥 노동자의 삶과는 다른 방향에서 역사의 현장을 목도하게 되는데, 1970년 《조선일보》 신춘문예 당선작인 「탑」은 이러한 폭넓은 시각에서 미제국주의를 고발하고 있는 작품이다. 또한 이때의 베트남 참전 경험은 「낙타누깔」(1972), 「몰개월의 새」(1976), 장편 『무기의 그늘』(1983) 등의 작품으로 그의 작품 세계를 풍요롭게 한다. 「탑」을 통해 거

short story, "Around Ipsok," a story based on his experience as a member of rock-climbing club in his high school. As a member of a teen intellectual circle together with other "rebels without cause," Hwang dipped into the works of great authors.

In 1964, during college, Hwang participated in students' demonstration against the Korean-Japanese Conference, got arrested and detained in the police station in Noryangjin, where he met a day laborer that was working at the construction site of the Second Hangang Bridge. Accompanying him, Hwang wandered around and worked at various construction sites including the site of a land-reclaiming project and a construction site in Shintanjin. This was probably the beginning of his career of wandering in the very bottom layer of our society. When Hwang settled as a novice monk at the Kumgangwon Temple after recklessly wandering all over the country, his mother found him and took him back home. Even after this incident, he again left home and wandered here and there, until finally he joined the Marine Corps in 1966 and was dispatched to Vietnam the next year. Based on this experience of participating in the war and witnessing a different kind of historical scene than

의 십 년에 가까운 문학적 공백기를 단숨에 메우면서 재기에 성공한 작가는 이때부터 황석영이라는 필명을 사용하면서 새로운 도약을 준비한다. 그리고 그해 전태일의 분신에 충격을 받고 「객지」를 구상, 집필하여 1971년 《창작과 비평》 봄호에 발표하게 된다. 파업 투쟁을 둘러싼 노동자들의 삶의 현장과 투지를 그린 이 작품으로 황석영은 많은 독자와 평자들로부터 찬사를 받고 '문제적인 작가'로 주목받는다. 이 작품의 결말에서 주인공 동혁이 '꼭 내일이 아니라도 좋다'라고 다짐하던 문구는 이후 70년대 한국 노동운동에 아포리즘으로 널리 퍼지고, 이후 민중들의 밑바닥 삶을 다룬 일련의 작품들을 발표하면서 작가 황석영은 70년대 리얼리즘을 대표하는 작가로 떠오른다. 황석영은 「객지」(1971), 「돼지꿈」(1973), 「장사의 꿈」(1974) 등을 통해 산업사회로 진입한 한국 사회 어두운 현실을 탁월하게 형상화하여 한국 민중문학의 새로운 지평을 열어젖히는 동시에 분단 현실에도 눈을 돌려 리얼리스트로서의 작가적 기량과 폭을 확대해 나간다. 1972년 한영기라는 의사의 일대기를 통해 분단된 민족의 비극과 모순을 그려 낸 중편 「한씨 연대기」를 발표한 후, 현실에 밀착된 그의 글쓰기는 또다시 노동 현실로 침투해 들어간다.

that of day laborers, his short story, "Pagoda," the winner of the *Chosun-ilbo* Spring literary Contest, contains a sharp criticism of the American imperialism. He published many more works, based on his experience of the Vietnam War, including "Camel Eye" (1972), "Bird of Molgaewol" (1976) and the novel *The Shadow of Arms* (1983). After making a successful comeback through "Pagoda," Hwang began a new phase of his writing career, adopting a pseudonym Hwang Sok-yong. Shocked at the Chŏn Tae-il Self-immolation Incident in 1970, he published "Away From Home" in the quarterly literary magazine *Ch'angjag-gwa-Bipyŏng (Creation and Criticism)* the next year. This story drew praises from both critics and the reading public for its realistic depiction of lives and struggles of day laborers during their strike, establishing Hwang as one of the most important writers of this period. The concluding remark by its main character Tong-hyok, "It's ok even if it's not tomorrow," became the aphorism of the 1970's labor movement, and Hwang became one of the most representative realists of the 1970's after publishing more stories dealing with lives of marginalized people. While Hwang superbly depicted the darker side of Korean society during

1973년 그는 구로공단 연합노조준비위를 구성하여 공장에 취업하게 되는데, 이때 겪은 민중의 삶을 황석영은 「잡초」, 「야근」, 「삼포 가는 길」, 「섬섬옥수」(1973) 등과 같은 단편을 통해 미적으로 형상화할 뿐 아니라 「구로공단의 노동 실태」(1973)와 같은 르포를 통해 고발한다. 초기 황석영의 작가적 행보는 주로 리얼리스트로서 크게 주목 받아 온 것이 사실이지만, 놀라운 현실 투시력과 밀착력에 못지않게 아름다운 서정성과 비극적 낭만성으로 내장하고 있어 문학적으로도 뛰어난 성취를 보여 준다.

1974년에 이르러 황석영 문학은 또 한 번의 전환과 도약을 맞게 되는데, 장편 『장길산』 착수가 바로 그것이다. 조선조 숙종 연간에 황해도 구월산을 본거지로 활약한 의적패의 이야기를 축으로 당시의 사회상을 민중사적 시각에 담은 『장길산』은 1974년 7월부터 1984년 7월까지 십 년 동안 《한국일보》에 연재한 대하소설이다. 『장길산』은 단순한 옛날이야기가 아니라 과거 역사를 빌어, 당대 경제적 불평등과 정치적 억압 등을 비판하고 민중의 건강한 생명력과 전망을 담은 역사소설로, 놀라운 입담과 스케일을 통해 재미와 감동을 줌으로써 70, 80년대 한국 문학사에 한 획을 긋는 작품으로 평가받는다.

the period of rapid industrialization, he also published stories about the division of the country. After publishing the *Chronicle of Mr. Han,* a novella in which he depicted the tragedy and contradiction resulting from the division of the country through the story of a doctor named Han Yong-gi, Hwang turned his attention back to the reality of laborers. In 1973, he worked as a factory worker as a member of the Association of Kuro Industrial Complex Labor Unions Planning Committee, which resulted not only in such short stories as "Weeds," "Nightshift," "Road to Sampo," and "Delicate Hands" (1973) but also a report entitled "The True Condition of Labor in the Kuro Industrial Complex." Hwang's stories in this early period are known for their realistic depiction of the lives of marginalized people, but they show superb aesthetic achievement as well in their lyricism and tragic romanticism.

In 1974, Hwang attempted at another phase and a new challenge by beginning to serialize *Chang Gil-san,* a lengthy historical novel, in the newspaper *Hanguk-ilbo.* This novel deals with the society during the reign of King Sugjong from the perspective of ordinary people through the story of a

황석영은 한국의 대표적인 리얼리스트 작가이면서 동시에 노동운동가, 문화운동가, 반체제 인사이자 통일운동가, 민주 투사 등의 여러 가지 이름을 지닌 '실천가'이기도 한데, 그의 글 또한 소설이라는 미학적 장르만이 아니라 르포 및 고발문학 등의 다양한 형태로 표출된다. 1974년 황석영은 사북 탄광을 방문하여 그곳 실태를 담은 『벽지의 하늘』을 써 내고, 공단 여성 근로자의 삶을 취재한 『잃어버린 순이』를 발표한다. 같은 해 군사 정권의 유신 체제에 반대하는 저항 운동에 몸을 담으면서 '자유실천문인협회'를 주도적으로 창설하고 현장문화 운동 조직위에 참여한다.

1976년 황석영은 『장길산』 집필을 위해 가족과 함께 전남 해남으로 이주하는데, 그곳에서 창작에 몰두하는 한편, 전통 연희인 마당극을 기획하고 농민들과 어울려 농민운동을 펼친다. 황석영의 문화운동 실천은 문화패 '광대' 창설과 '민중문화연구소' 설립 등으로 계속되다가 광주 항쟁에 이르러 더욱 증폭된다. 제주와 광주 등을 거치면서 광주 항쟁의 진상을 알리고 독재 정권 타도에 앞장서던 작가는 1985년 광주항쟁 기록을 담은 『죽음을 넘어, 시대의 어둠을 넘어』를 비밀리에 출판한다. 이 책은 한국 민주화

band of righteous outlaws led by Chang Gil-san and headquartered in Mount Kuwol in Hwanghae-do. Although a historical novel, this saga is not simply a story of the past but a story that has implications in the present, especially in terms of its economic inequality and political oppression. It was a significant literary achievement of the 1970's and 1980's in that it highlights healthy vitality and historical viewpoint of ordinary people and that it does this through a deeply moving and enjoyable story narrated in a prose with great conversational power.

Not only a novelist but also an activist working for labor, culture, democracy, and unification movements as well as a political dissident, Hwang published many reports on the contemporary social conditions including "Sky of the Remote Place" (1974), a report on the mine in Sabuk and "Sun-i Lost" (1974), a report on the lives of female factory workers. The same year, he also actively participated in the founding of the Writers' Council for Freedom and Action and in the organizing committee of a field cultural movement.

In 1976, Hwang moved to Haenam, Chŏllanam-do with his family in order to concentrate on the

운동에 중대한 영향을 끼친 글로 작가로서의 명성뿐 아니라 투사로서의 황석영의 실천적 면모를 드높인 '저술'이었다.

1985년 작가 황석영은 서부 독일 베를린에서 열린 '제3세계 문화제'에 아시아 대표로 참가하여 유럽, 미국, 일본 등지를 돌며 '통일굿'을 공연하고 바깥 세계로 점차 시야를 넓혀 간다. 그리하여 황석영은 민족 국가 내부의 모순뿐 아니라 그것이 놓여 있는 보다 더 큰 국제 정세와 한반도에 눈을 돌리게 되는데, 이러한 또 한 번의 전환기를 보여 주는 것이 1989년의 방북이다. 당시 한국 사회에 충격적인 파문을 일으켰던 이 방북 사건은 그를 작가가 아니라 '반체제 인사'로 바꿔 놓았고, 황석영은 귀국하지 못하고 베를린과 미국 등의 국경 바깥을 떠돌게 된다. 그는 해외에서 남·북·해외 동포가 망라된 '조국통일범민족연합'을 창립하는 등 통일운동을 하는 한편, 북한 방문기 『사람이 살고 있었네』를 국내 잡지에 연재한다. 해외 체류 기간 동안 황석영은 베를린 장벽의 붕괴와 동구 사회주의권의 몰락과 해체를 목격하고 또 한 번의 문학적 전환점을 향해 나아간다.

황석영은 망명과 추방으로 이어지는 해외 생활을 청산

writing of *Chang Gil-san*. In Haenam, while he was working on *Chang Gil-san*, he also participated in the peasant movement, working on madang-guk, traditional Korean drama, with peasants. Hwang continued to participate in the cultural movement, founding and establishing the drama troop, Kwangdae, and the Institute for People's Culture. After the Kwangju Uprising in 1980, he secretly published *Beyond Death, Beyond the Darkness of Our Time*, a book that records the truth of the Kwangju Uprising. This book had a great influence on the Korean democracy movement, highlighting Hwang not only as author but also as activist.

In 1985, Hwang Sok-yong attended the Third World Culture Festival in Berlin, West Germany, as a representative of Asia and led a tour of the performance, "Unification Gut," in Europe, the US, and Japan. This offered an occasion for Hwang to see the challenges that people were facing in the Korean peninsula in the bigger context of international geopolitics, which led him to his illegal visit to North Korea in 1989. This incident that shocked the entire South Korean society turned him from an author into a political dissident, who could not return home, and he wandered around the US and

하고 1993년 4월 귀국한다. 고국에 돌아온 그는 방북 사건으로 징역 칠 년형을 선고받고 오랜 수감 생활에 들어간다. 첫 삼 년 동안 그는 근엄한 정치범의 투쟁적 자세로 '옥살이'를 견디다 나중에는 잡범들과 교유하며 생활인으로서의 '맷집'을 다져 간다. 1998년 사면되어 감옥에서 나온 그는 다시 창작에 몰두한다. 반체제 인사의 비극적 삶을 그린 『오래된 정원』(1999)과 파행적인 한국 근대사의 비극을 그린 『손님』(2001)을 신문에 연재하면서 왕성한 문학 활동을 재개한 황석영은 그의 문학적 연대기를 새롭게 써 나가기 시작한다. 『손님』과 더불어 『심청』(2003)과 『바리데기』(2007)에 이르기까지 출옥 이후 그의 작품은 주로 세계 보편적 시각에서 한국 근대사와 세계 난민들의 실상을 담아내고 있는데, 특이한 것은 이러한 일련의 작품들이 한국의 고유한 전통 양식, 즉 굿이나 설화 등을 차용하여 새롭게 변용하고 있다는 것이다. 1962년 등단 이후 거센 현실의 물살 속에 몸을 담고 현실과 정면 대결함으로써 독보적인 문학 세계를 열어 왔던 작가 황석영의 필력은 여전히 진행 중이다.

Germany. During this period of wandering, he was involved in the overseas reunification movement, establishing the Pan-Korean Alliance for Reunification, while serializing *There Lived People*, a book on his travel to North Korea, in a Korean magazine. He also witnessed the fall of the Berlin Wall as well as the collapse of the Eastern European regimes, which prepared him for a new literary phase.

Hwang returned home in 1993 after a long period of exile and was imprisoned for a long time after receiving a seven-year sentence. For the first three years, he sternly endured his imprisonment in a fashion characteristic to a feisty political prisoner, but later, he associated with petty criminals, again learning about the way of life of the ordinary people. Hwang was released in 1998, after being granted an amnesty, and enthusiastically resumed fiction writing, serializing *Old Garden* (1999), a story about a tragic life of a dissident, and *Guest* (2001), a novel on the tragic development of modern Korean history, in a newspaper. Hwang's recent novels, including the more recent *Shim Ch'ŏng* (2003) and *Paridegi* (2007), deal with modern Korean history and the problem of migrant workers from the perspective of contemporary world history. Interestingly, Hwang adopted traditional forms of Korean culture such as gut and folktale in these novels with international overtones. Hwang Sok-yong, who created his own unique world of literature by resolutely confronting the harsh reality of his country and the world since his debut in 1962, is still an author in active service.

번역 **김우창** Translated by Kim U-chang

서울대학교 영어영문학과와 미국 코넬 대학교 대학원을 거쳐 하버드 대학교에서 미국 문명사 박사 학위를 받았다. 서울대학교와 고려대학교에서 영어영문학과 교수를 지냈고, 현재 고려대학교 명예교수이며 이화여자대학교 학술원 석좌교수로 있다. 1965년 《청맥》 지에 「엘리어트의 예(例)」로 등단한 문학평론가이자 영문학자이다. 저서로는 『김우창 전집』과 『심미적 이성의 탐구』 『정치와 삶의 세계』 『행동과 사유』 『사유의 공간』 『시대의 흐름에 서서』 『풍경과 마음』 등이 있다. 『한국 문학 선집—고대에서 근대 이전까지』 『한국 현대 문학—박목월 시 선집』 등 다수의 한국 문학을 번역했다.

Kim U-chang was born in 1937, in Hampyung, Korea. He is currently a Professor Emeritus at Korea University and a chair professor in the Academy of Advanced Studies in Ewha Womans University. He made his literary debut in 1965 with the critique "The Formality of Eliot" His major works include *The Poet in Time of Need* (1977), *Measure on Earth* (1981), *Studies in Aesthetic Reason* (1992), *The Poet's Stone* (1993), *The Lawless Road* (1993), *Towards a Rational Society* (1993), *Justice and Its Conditions* (2008), *Venn Diagram's Three Circles [dialogues]* (2008) He has published numerous translations of Korean literature including *Anthology of Korean Literature: From Early Times to the Nineteenth Century, Modern Korean Literature: An Anthology, Pak Mogwol's Selected Poems.*

감수 K. E. 더핀 Edited by K. E. Duffin

시인, 화가, 판화가. 하버드 인문대학원 글쓰기 지도 강사를 역임하고, 현재 프리랜서 에디터, 글쓰기 컨설턴트로 활동하고 있다.

K. E. Duffin is a poet, painter and printmaker. She is currently working as a freelance editor and writing consultant as well. She was a writing tutor for the Graduate School of Arts and Sciences, Harvard University.

감수 **전승희** Edited by Jeon Seung-hee

번역문학가, 문학평론가. 하버드대학교 한국학연구소 연구원으로 재직 중이며 바흐친의 『장편소설과 민중언어』, 제인 오스틴의 『오만과 편견』 등을 공역했다.

Jeon Seung-hee is a literary critic and translator. She is currently a fellow at the Korea Institute, Harvard University. Her translations include Mikhail Bakhtin's *Novel and the People's Culture* and Jane Austen's *Pride and Prejudice.*

바이링궐 에디션 한국 대표 소설 007
삼포 가는 길

2012년 7월 25일 초판 1쇄 발행
2020년 4월 20일 초판 4쇄 발행

지은이 황석영 | **옮긴이** 김우창 | **펴낸이** 김재범
감수 K. E. Duffin, Jeon Seung-hee | **기획위원** 전성태, 정은경, 이경재
편집 강민영, 김지연 | **관리** 박수연, 홍희표 | **디자인** 나루기획
인쇄·제책 굿에그커뮤니케이션 | **종이** 한솔PNS
펴낸곳 (주)아시아 | **출판등록** 2006년 1월 27일 제406-2006-000004호
주소 경기도 파주시 회동길 445(서울 사무소: 서울특별시 동작구 서달로 161-1 3층)
전화 02.821.5055 | **팩스** 02.821.5057 | **홈페이지** www.bookasia.org
ISBN 978-89-94006-20-8 (set) | 978-89-94006-26-0 (04810)
값은 뒤표지에 있습니다.

Bi-lingual Edition Modern Korean Literature 007
The Road to Sampo

Written by Hwang Sok-yong | **Translated by** Kim U-ch'ang
Published by Asia Publishers | 445, Hoedong-gil, Paju-si, Gyeonggi-do, Korea
(Seoul Office: 161-1, Seodal-ro, Dongjak-gu, Seoul, Korea)
Homepage Address www.bookasia.org | **Tel**. (822).821.5055 | **Fax**. (822).821.5057
First published in Korea by Asia Publishers 2012
ISBN 978-89-94006-20-8 (set) | 978-89-94006-26-0 (04810)

바이링궐 에디션 한국 대표 소설

한국문학의 가장 중요하고 첨예한 문제의식을 가진 작가들의 대표작을 주제별로 선정!
하버드 한국학 연구원 및 세계 각국의 한국문학 전문 번역진이 참여한 번역 시리즈!
미국 하버드대학교와 컬럼비아대학교 동아시아학과, 캐나다 브리티시컬럼비아대학교 아시아학과 등 해외 대학에서 교재로 채택!

바이링궐 에디션 한국 대표 소설 set 1

분단 Division

01 병신과 머저리-**이청준** The Wounded-**Yi Cheong-jun**
02 어둠의 혼-**김원일** Soul of Darkness-**Kim Won-il**
03 순이삼촌-**현기영** Sun-i Samch'on-**Hyun Ki-young**
04 엄마의 말뚝 1-**박완서** Mother's Stake I-**Park Wan-suh**
05 유형의 땅-**조정래** The Land of the Banished-**Jo Jung-rae**

산업화 Industrialization

06 무진기행-**김승옥** Record of a Journey to Mujin-**Kim Seung-ok**
07 삼포 가는 길-**황석영** The Road to Sampo-**Hwang Sok-yong**
08 아홉 켤레의 구두로 남은 사내-**윤흥길** The Man Who Was Left as Nine Pairs of Shoes-**Yun Heung-gil**
09 돌아온 우리의 친구-**신상웅** Our Friend's Homecoming-**Shin Sang-ung**
10 원미동 시인-**양귀자** The Poet of Wŏnmi-dong-**Yang Kwi-ja**

여성 Women

11 중국인 거리-**오정희** Chinatown-**Oh Jung-hee**
12 풍금이 있던 자리-**신경숙** The Place Where the Harmonium Was-**Shin Kyung-sook**
13 하나코는 없다-**최윤** The Last of Hanak'o-**Ch'oe Yun**
14 인간에 대한 예의-**공지영** Human Decency-**Gong Ji-young**
15 빈처-**은희경** Poor Man's Wife-**Eun Hee-kyung**

바이링궐 에디션 한국 대표 소설 set 2

자유 Liberty

16 필론의 돼지-**이문열** Pilon's Pig-**Yi Mun-yol**
17 슬로우 불릿-**이대환** Slow Bullet-**Lee Dae-hwan**
18 직선과 독가스-**임철우** Straight Lines and Poison Gas-**Lim Chul-woo**
19 깃발-**홍희담** The Flag-**Hong Hee-dam**
20 새벽 출정-**방현석** Off to Battle at Dawn-**Bang Hyeon-seok**

사랑과 연애 Love and Love Affairs

21 별을 사랑하는 마음으로-**윤후명** With the Love for the Stars-**Yun Hu-myong**
22 목련공원-**이승우** Magnolia Park-**Lee Seung-u**
23 칼에 찔린 자국-**김인숙** Stab-**Kim In-suk**
24 회복하는 인간-**한강** Convalescence-**Han Kang**
25 트렁크-**정이현** In the Trunk-**Jeong Yi-hyun**

남과 북 South and North

26 판문점-**이호철** Panmunjom-**Yi Ho-chol**
27 수난 이대-**하근찬** The Suffering of Two Generations-**Ha Geun-chan**
28 분지-**남정현** Land of Excrement-**Nam Jung-hyun**
29 봄 실상사-**정도상** Spring at Silsangsa Temple-**Jeong Do-sang**
30 은행나무 사랑-**김하기** Gingko Love-**Kim Ha-kee**

바이링궐 에디션 한국 대표 소설 set 3

서울 Seoul

31 눈사람 속의 검은 항아리-**김소진** The Dark Jar within the Snowman-**Kim So-jin**
32 오후, 가로지르다-**하성란** Traversing Afternoon-**Ha Seong-nan**
33 나는 봉천동에 산다-**조경란** I Live in Bongcheon-dong-**Jo Kyung-ran**
34 그렇습니까? 기린입니다-**박민규** Is That So? I'm A Giraffe-**Park Min-gyu**
35 성탄특선-**김애란** Christmas Specials-**Kim Ae-ran**

전통 Tradition

36 무자년의 가을 사흘-**서정인** Three Days of Autumn, 1948-**Su Jung-in**
37 유자소전-**이문구** A Brief Biography of Yuja-**Yi Mun-gu**
38 향기로운 우물 이야기-**박범신** The Fragrant Well-**Park Bum-shin**
39 월행-**송기원** A Journey under the Moonlight-**Song Ki-won**
40 협죽도 그늘 아래-**성석제** In the Shade of the Oleander-**Song Sok-ze**

아방가르드 Avant-garde

41 아겔다마-**박상륭** Akeldama-**Park Sang-ryoong**
42 내 영혼의 우물-**최인석** A Well in My Soul-**Choi In-seok**
43 당신에 대해서-**이인성** On You-**Yi In-seong**
44 회색 時-**배수아** Time In Gray-**Bae Su-ah**
45 브라운 부인-**정영문** Mrs. Brown-**Jung Young-moon**

바이링궐 에디션 한국 대표 소설 set 4

디아스포라 Diaspora

46 속옷-**김남일** Underwear-**Kim Nam-il**
47 상하이에 두고 온 사람들-**공선옥** People I Left in Shanghai-**Gong Sun-ok**
48 모두에게 복된 새해-**김연수** Happy New Year to Everyone-**Kim Yeon-su**
49 코끼리-**김재영** The Elephant-**Kim Jae-young**
50 먼지별-**이경** Dust Star-**Lee Kyung**

가족 Family

51 혜자의 눈꽃-**천승세** Hye-ja's Snow-Flowers-**Chun Seung-sei**
52 아베의 가족-**전상국** Ahbe's Family-**Jeon Sang-guk**
53 문 앞에서-**이동하** Outside the Door-**Lee Dong-ha**
54 그리고, 축제-**이혜경** And Then the Festival-**Lee Hye-kyung**
55 봄밤-**권여선** Spring Night-**Kwon Yeo-sun**

유머 Humor

56 오늘의 운세-**한창훈** Today's Fortune-**Han Chang-hoon**
57 새-**전성태** Bird-**Jeon Sung-tae**
58 밀수록 다시 가까워지는-**이기호** So Far, and Yet So Near-**Lee Ki-ho**
59 유리방패-**김중혁** The Glass Shield-**Kim Jung-hyuk**
60 전당포를 찾아서-**김종광** The Pawnshop Chase-**Kim Chong-kwang**

바이링궐 에디션 한국 대표 소설 set 5

관계 Relationship

61 도둑견습 – **김주영** Robbery Training-**Kim Joo-young**
62 사랑하라, 희망 없이 – **윤영수** Love, Hopelessly-**Yun Young-su**
63 봄날 오후, 과부 셋 – **정지아** Spring Afternoon, Three Widows-**Jeong Ji-a**
64 유턴 지점에 보물지도를 묻다 – **윤성희** Burying a Treasure Map at the U-turn-**Yoon Sung-hee**
65 쁘이거나 쯔이거나 – **백가흠** Puy, Thuy, Whatever-**Paik Ga-huim**

일상의 발견 Discovering Everyday Life

66 나는 음식이다 – **오수연** I Am Food-**Oh Soo-yeon**
67 트럭 – **강영숙** Truck-**Kang Young-sook**
68 통조림 공장 – **편혜영** The Canning Factory-**Pyun Hye-young**
69 꽃 – **부희령** Flowers-**Pu Hee-ryoung**
70 피의일요일 – **윤이형** Bloody Sunday-**Yun I-hyeong**

금기와 욕망 Taboo and Desire

71 북소리 - **송영** Drumbeat-**Song Yong**
72 발칸의 장미를 내게 주었네 - **정미경** He Gave Me Roses of the Balkans-**Jung Mi-kyung**
73 아무도 돌아오지 않는 밤 - **김숨** The Night Nobody Returns Home-**Kim Soom**
74 젓가락여자 - **천운영** Chopstick Woman-**Cheon Un-yeong**
75 아직 일어나지 않은 일 - **김미월** What Has Yet to Happen-**Kim Mi-wol**

바이링궐 에디션 한국 대표 소설 set 6

운명 Fate

76 언니를 놓치다 - **이경자** Losing a Sister-**Lee Kyung-ja**
77 아들 - **윤정모** Father and Son-**Yoon Jung-mo**
78 명두 - **구효서** Relics-**Ku Hyo-seo**
79 모독 - **조세희** Insult-**Cho Se-hui**
80 화요일의 강 - **손홍규** Tuesday River-**Son Hong-gyu**

미의 사제들 Aesthetic Priests

81 고수 - **이외수** Grand Master-**Lee Oisoo**
82 말을 찾아서 - **이순원** Looking for a Horse-**Lee Soon-won**
83 상춘곡 - **윤대녕** Song of Everlasting Spring-**Youn Dae-nyeong**
84 삭매와 자미 - **김별아** Sakmae and Jami-**Kim Byeol-ah**
85 저만치 혼자서 - **김훈** Alone Over There-**Kim Hoon**

식민지의 벌거벗은 자들 The Naked in the Colony

86 감자 - **김동인** Potatoes-**Kim Tong-in**
87 운수 좋은 날 - **현진건** A Lucky Day-**Hyŏn Chin'gŏn**
88 탈출기 - **최서해** Escape-**Ch'oe So-hae**
89 과도기 - **한설야** Transition-**Han Seol-ya**
90 지하촌 - **강경애** The Underground Village-**Kang Kyŏng-ae**

바이링궐 에디션 한국 대표 소설 set 7

백치가 된 식민지 지식인 Colonial Intellectuals Turned "Idiots"

91 날개 - **이상** Wings-**Yi Sang**
92 김 강사와 T 교수 - **유진오** Lecturer Kim and Professor T-**Chin-O Yu**
93 소설가 구보씨의 일일 - **박태원** A Day in the Life of Kubo the Novelist-**Pak Taewon**
94 비 오는 길 - **최명익** Walking in the Rain-**Ch'oe Myŏngik**
95 빛 속에 - **김사량** Into the Light-**Kim Sa-ryang**

한국의 잃어버린 얼굴 Traditional Korea's Lost Faces

96 봄·봄 – **김유정** Spring, Spring–**Kim Yu-jeong**
97 벙어리 삼룡이 – **나도향** Samnyong the Mute–**Na Tohyang**
98 달밤 – **이태준** An Idiot's Delight–**Yi T'ae-jun**
99 사랑손님과 어머니 – **주요섭** Mama and the Boarder–**Chu Yo-sup**
100 갯마을 – **오영수** Seaside Village–**Oh Yeongsu**

해방 전후(前後) Before and After Liberation

101 소망 – **채만식** Juvesenility–**Ch'ae Man-Sik**
102 두 파산 – **염상섭** Two Bankruptcies–**Yom Sang-Seop**
103 풀잎 – **이효석** Leaves of Grass–**Lee Hyo-seok**
104 맥 – **김남천** Barley–**Kim Namch'on**
105 꺼삐딴 리 – **전광용** Kapitan Ri–**Chŏn Kwangyong**

전후(戰後) Korea After the Korean War

106 소나기 – **황순원** The Cloudburst–**Hwang Sun-Won**
107 등신불 – **김동리** Tŭngsin-bul–**Kim Tong-ni**
108 요한 시집 – **장용학** The Poetry of John–**Chang Yong-hak**
109 비 오는 날 – **손창섭** Rainy Days–**Son Chang-sop**
110 오발탄 – **이범선** A Stray Bullet–**Lee Beomseon**

K-픽션 한국 젊은 소설

최근에 발표된 단편소설 중 가장 우수하고 흥미로운 작품을 엄선하여 출간하는 〈K-픽션〉은 한국문학의 생생한 현장을 국내외 독자들과 실시간으로 공유하고자 기획되었습니다. 원작의 재미와 품격을 최대한 살린 〈K-픽션〉 시리즈는 매 계절마다 새로운 작품을 선보입니다.

001 버핏과의 저녁 식사-**박민규** Dinner with Buffett-**Park Min-gyu**
002 아르판-**박형서** Arpan-**Park hyoung su**
003 애드벌룬-**손보미** Hot Air Balloon-**Son Bo-mi**
004 나의 클린트 이스트우드-**오한기** My Clint Eastwood-**Oh Han-ki**
005 이베리아의 전갈-**최민우** Dishonored-**Choi Min-woo**
006 양의 미래-**황정은** Kong's Garden-**Hwang Jung-eun**
007 대니-**윤이형** Danny-**Yun I-hyeong**
008 퇴근-**천명관** Homecoming-**Cheon Myeong-kwan**
009 옥화-**금희** Ok-hwa-**Geum Hee**
010 시차-**백수린** Time Difference-**Baik Sou linne**
011 올드 맨 리버-**이장욱** Old Man River-**Lee Jang-wook**
012 권순찬과 착한 사람들-**이기호** Kwon Sun-chan and Nice People-**Lee Ki-ho**
013 알바생 자르기-**장강명** Fired-**Chang Kangmyoung**
014 어디로 가고 싶으신가요-**김애란** Where Would You Like To Go?-**Kim Ae-ran**
015 세상에서 가장 비싼 소설-**김민정** The World's Most Expensive Novel-**Kim Min-jung**
016 체스의 모든 것-**김금희** Everything About Chess-**Kim Keum-hee**
017 할로윈-**정한아** Halloween-**Chung Han-ah**
018 그 여름-**최은영** The Summer-**Choi Eunyoung**
019 어느 피씨주의자의 종생기-**구병모** The Story of P.C.-**Gu Byeong-mo**
020 모르는 영역-**권여선** An Unknown Realm-**Kwon Yeo-sun**
021 4월의 눈-**손원평** April Snow-**Sohn Won-pyung**
022 서우-**강화길** Seo-u-**Kang Hwa-gil**
023 가출-**조남주** Run Away-**Cho Nam-joo**
024 연애의 감정학-**백영옥** How to Break Up Like a Winner-**Baek Young-ok**
025 창모-**우다영** Chang-mo-**Woo Da-young**
026 검은 방-**정지아** The Black Room-**Jeong Ji-a**